THE KISS OF LIFE

The Impossible Romance

Copyright © 2021

The Kiss Of Life

The impossible romance

Copyright © 2021 by (Donna Tischner)

Dfortissimo@aol.com

All rights reserved. No part of this book may be reproduced or transmitted in any form or by any means without written permission from the author.

First Edition, April 2021

Donna Tischner

All rights reserved. 2021

ISBN: 9798738718595

The Kiss Of Life

The Impossible Romance:

SUMMARY

In the darkness of one rural town lives amongst them, a creature from the cold world—Romanian searches for that extraordinary mortal, with her divine blood for powers beyond imagination.

His ruthlessness and indifferent behavior towards her are unmerciful.

She is torn between love and hate for him.

He is torn between her blood and eternal beauty.

When the kiss of life is upon her, she finds that this impossible romance has an enduring edge of passion, power, and strength to no avail.

And their love is under the abomination of the shadowy mystique.

Donna Tischner

Thank you to my family, for putting up with
me these past couple of months.
For all the late-night dinners, and salads you had to eat,
and for listening to my music on constant repeat. (LOL)

"THE BLOOD FOREVER BINDS THE KISS OF LIFE."

dt

Donna Tischner
Email: Dfortissimo@aol.com

"REVENGE IS SWEET." • "BLOOD IS THE LIFE …

ROMANIAN VLAD III

ACKNOWLEDGMENTS

I'd like to thank, Asdrall, our cover model for his amazing look.
For more information on Asdrall, please visit his web page at,
https://asdrall.wixsite.com/uriel

I'd also like to thank,
Renu Sharma, for her amazing artwork, on
Our Cover Jacket.
For more information on Renu, please visit her webpage.
Renu Sharma | @thedarkrayne

Much love to you both, thank you again
for helping me bring my book to life.

Kiss Of Life

Chapter 1:
THE DRIVE

Receiving that phone call last week really hurt. My father was my hero.

Now I leave Manhattan to go back home. I take the long trip by myself, Upstate NY, down the long cold highway, when my mind takes me back to all those childhood memories with my family.

Is it just me, or is the winter more depressing than the other seasons?

I put the radio on, listening to all my favorite pop songs. Hoping it will cheer me up.

I open the window a crack, and my long dark hair blows, whipping me in the face, remembering when my dad taught me how to ride a bike, and my hair kept flying in my eyes.

The tears start building up. Reminiscing when my father built me my first playhouse with working doors and windows. My friends and I played in there all day long.

Donna Tischner

Life seemed so much easier back then.

As these big trucks pass me on the road, my Jeep gets a gust of wind and blows gently to the side. I put my signal on to move out of their way.
Continuing down the highway, my exit comes up fast, and I get off. Turning into the police station. I park... Getting out of the jeep, I walk into the building.

When my father's fellow officers greet me, saying how sorry they are about my dad's passing. They Pat me on the back as I pass them. Saying, "Call them, if I need anything." I smile and make my way to the Sergeant's office.

I knock on the door, and he yell's, "Come in." When he sees me, he stands from his seat and quickly rushes to my side, holding me. Telling me, he's so sorry about my father, and what a great detective he was.

I cry in his chest as he rubs the back of my hair, then, wrapping his arms around me.

I tell Mr. Butler, "Thank you, that means a lot to me." Then he asks me to have a seat. He begins by saying,

Kiss Of Life

"Your father's death is a mystery, and we are still investigating, even the crime scene; we have a few leads, but nothing solid, I'm sorry Jewel's, there were no marks on him and nothing near his body when we found him. We called in all the best crime scene investigators and Forensic analysts."

Then Mr. Butler bends down and picks up a box from under his desk, it is all my father's belongings from his office. I take out a picture, staring at it. It's one of him and all his buddies from the station. And another one of me. He's kissing me on my cheek in the picture.

More tears, and I need to sit.

Mr. Butler assures me he will be in touch with me as soon as they have a lead, then I walk out of his office, proceeding to the exit.

I put the box in the back and get in the driver's seat, put my hands on the steering wheel and begin weeping. I turn on the engine and drive to my childhood home. I start remembering when my mother passed some years ago from a pneumonia, and my dad was devastated. Now I'm all alone and leaving Manhattan to come home to take care of our family house. I still don't know if I'm going to sell it or keep it. But right now, I plan to stay there until

I figure things out.

As the evening sets, light illuminates from the mountains. I still have sunlight to get settled in as I pull into the driveway. Seeing our tan L-shaped house, I get out of the truck with my father's manicured lawn and look around my old neighborhood.

With all the new additions to the block, some of the neighbors, had extensions added on, a couple of new homes had been built, and how clean everything seems, except for that huge Victorian house on the corner. It's just across the street from our house.

It's large, wide, and gray in color. The trees and shrubs are all overgrown. Growing in between the tall black rod iron fence, vines. The shingles are falling off and the paint is chipped. *It looks haunted.*

I look up at the window, of the second floor and see a man. Staring down at me behind the drapes. He lets me know he sees me. *Creepy*, I think to myself.

I pull a few boxes out of the truck and carry them to the front door. I put the key in and unlock it, sliding my hand up against the wall looking for the light switch, and turning it on. I put the boxes down and go back outside to get my clothes, and I see that man again, still looking down at me. I close the back hatch and go inside, locking the doors.

Kiss Of Life

I sit on the sofa and look around the room at all my parent's belongings. A few minutes later, I stand, thinking about the guy in the window. I walk over to my window moving the blinds to see if anyone is out there. When I see him still standing there, wondering what he's doing, I walk away.

I stroll down the hall and turn on every light because I'm a little scared of being alone right now. It's been five years since I've been home.

When I was leaving for school in Manhattan, that man was moving in. I have never seen him or got to know him.

I make the house noisy by putting on some of my dad's music, playing Sinatra and other oldies he loved. It brings me comfort, and I enjoy remembering him singing to this.

I begin to sing too, and I feel the wetness in my eyes, but I continue to sing and unpack my clothes. I decided to stay in my childhood bedroom while living here.

That's when I hear a noise outside and freeze. It sounds like leaves crunching when someone walks on them. I grab my cell phone and prepare to call 911. But the sound stops. I'm unsure if someone is just standing there or they

Donna Tischner

left.

    I look for a weapon in my bedroom, but all I can find is an empty wine bottle. I pick it up and begin to search the house. I checked the living room, the dining room, and kitchen, but I don't see anything out of the ordinary. I don't hear crunching leaves either anymore. I go back into my room and unpack the rest of my things.

    I place my perfumes on the dresser, brushes, and makeup. Grab my blow dryer and curling iron, putting them on the counter in the bathroom.
    Then I decide to go into the kitchen and find something to eat. I open the refrigerator and smell the milk, then put it back. I take out the eggs and check them too. Everything seems to be good. I make a sandwich and head into the living room, turning on the TV, and watch a show eating, and then I grab the afghan. Covering myself, I fall asleep on the couch.

    Then I hear a banging sound and I jump. Scared, I stand near the sofa waiting. Unsure, where the sound is coming from, I'm shaking. I feel my knees vibrating, I hold my dancing hands to keep them still, but I can still feel them jittering.

Kiss Of Life

I still don't know where that bang came from, but it sounded like it was in the house. I wait standing, for a few more seconds, then sit back down. My heart is racing from being so scared. I lean back on the sofa, trying to keep my eyes open, but I fall back to sleep.

Donna Tischner

CHAPTER 2:
GETTING REACQUAINTED

When I wake, I open all the blinds and the front door letting in some sunlight. That's when I see Mr. Michaels. My neighbor. He bends down at my front door and hands me a package. I open the door and invite him in, taking the box wrapped in brown paper from him. He says, " This was here when I walked up." "Thank you," I said. He asks how I've been and apologizes for my dad's passing. Then he asks me to have dinner with him and his family tonight. I accept his invitation. He leaves telling me to come at 4:00 p.m.

Then I stare at the strange package left on my doorstep, realizing that's what I heard last night, someone put the box there.

I decide to go outside and check the mailbox. While walking down the long walkway taking in the fresh air, I

Kiss Of Life

look at that Victorian, wondering why they never fixed it up or cleaned the grounds.

Then I hear someone yell out, "Good morning!" I look over and see my neighbor Mrs. Wilder. I said, "Good morning." She walks over to me. She is asking if I'm alright and apologizes about Dad's passing. I hug and kiss her, telling her I'm okay. We talk for a few minutes then another neighbor comes by, telling me how much they loved my father.

I begin to question them about the man that lives in the Victorian house—asking if he ever leaves or if they ever see him. They tell me they have never seen him and that he seems okay. He doesn't make any trouble.

Then they mention Memorial Day approaching, and they're having a Block party. I smile big, letting them know I will be attending.

I open the door to the mailbox and pull out all the many papers and letters. Then go into the house and see all the cards. I open three envelopes and see sympathy cards. It makes me upset, so I don't bother opening the rest.

I take the mail and move it into my father's office. While I'm in there, I sit in his office chair and rub my hand over his desk, feeling the shiny laminated wood. Then I decided to look in his draw's, finding some documents. I begin to read them. They read,

2 teenagers have been found dead near the East Point Lake, Cause of death, unknown. But two marks have been found on their necks. They appear to be snake bites.
I continue to read.
The coroner's report said these were not snake bites, and they are unsure what the two tiny marks can be.

I put the documents back in the draw and close it. Leaving his office and closing the door behind me. I stand with my back to his office door. Close my eyes and take a deep breath.

When I hear a banging sound coming from inside the house again. I freeze. Looking around me, turning my head to the left and then to the right. I don't see anything. The banging stops. Still, feeling uneasy, I check out parts of the house making sure no one is in here.

I didn't see anything unusual, so I go about my day.
I take my shower and prepare for tonight's dinner at Mr. Michaels. I go for a drive to the corner market and purchase some wine and cake for dessert. Then walk

Kiss Of Life

around town and shop for me. Some locals recognize me, saying hi, and asking how I am. Getting reacquainted with them, and they tell me, "welcome back." I smile shyly and drive home.

It's now 4:00 p.m. and I grab my desserts and begin to walk across the street to Mr. Michaels. When I see that man in the window again from the Victorian house, this time, he opens the drapes wide enough for me to view him more than before. It's as if he's saying, *"See Me!"* so I try to be polite, and I smile at him, continuing to walk. There is no reaction from him other than him dropping the curtains, and then he walks away.

I knock on Mr. Michaels door, and they greet me pleasantly with kisses, telling me to come in. They take the wine and open it, pouring me some, asking me to have a seat. Then the rest of the family comes in greeting me.

I mention the Victorian house on the corner to them, asking if they met the family there, but they tell me no, they never come out. Then I ask if they have jobs that they go to, but they just tell me, they're unsure. Mr. Michaels mentions that he thinks they have money, because they've seen a limousine pull into the garage at night a few times. And people dressed in fancy clothing come and

Donna Tischner

go during the night hours.

  Mrs. Michaels told me, a few times she heard girls screaming, like they were in trouble. It always sounds like it's coming from his corner. I sit there thinking about what that could have been, but I turn up no answer.
We talk more, eat then have cake and coffee. Now 8:00 p.m. I say my goodbyes and start to walk home.

  As I cross the street, a man from the Victorian house is pulling garbage cans to the road, and he sees me, stopping me to talk. I get startled. He tells me, "There's no need to be afraid. I'm not going to hurt you."

I look closer at the man, but he's not the same guy in the window. This man is shorter and more decadent. I say to the gentleman, "Can I help you?"

He starts to talk to me, saying, "My Master would like to get to know you. Would you be inclined to have an evening dinner with him?"

  Surprised by this, I answer,
" Um, when?"
"Tomorrow 8 p.m.?"
"Tomorrow? I don't think I can. I have somewhere to be."

Kiss Of Life

"Okay, I'll be sure to tell him you declined."
"But I didn't decline. I can't tomorrow night."

Then he walks away. I feel like I have just been beaten, and I don't know why. I go into my house and put the TV on, taking off my heels and jacket.

I look at the package that was left on my doorstep and decide to open it. I unwrap the brown paper and look at the cardboard box. Inside is an elegant brown marble box with a vast rose on top. I lift the lid and wrap in red tissue paper is a black blood brooch.

I hold the Pin in my hand, thinking how stunning it is but weird at the same time. I look back at the Card, and it reads, "Romanian Vlad the III, Welcome home."

Wondering who he is, I pin the brooch on my blouse.

Then make my way to my room to go to sleep.

By morning I get out of bed and sit on the edge, thinking about the brooch. I pick it up, still wondering who Romanian Vlad is. I put it down and head into the shower. I am going into town to inquire about work at the high school as a music teacher.

Donna Tischner

I pull out a pair of dressy black slacks and a cream color sweater top with a zipper down the front. Then grab my black heels, and resume. I pick up my keys and get into my Jeep. Driving down the road to the school. I walk through the school building for my interview, and flashbacks of my attending here ran through my mind when I was younger. *I laugh to myself.*

After the interview, I go to a friend for the night. Brook Winters and I have been friends since elementary school. She only lives down the road from me here. We have plans on going to a local club. We get dressed up, me in my black form-fitting above the knee-length dress, and off the shoulder.

I find the perfect spot over my breast for my new brooch.

Brook is wearing a blue dress that puffs out at the waist. We both do our hair. I'm wearing mine down with curls that flip back. Brook's hair is in an updo. Complimenting each other, we head out to the club.

Once there, we get our drinks, meeting our friends Jack and Kim, and take a seat in a booth. Observing everything that goes on around me, I notice a very distinguished

Kiss Of Life

gentleman going into the club's VIP section. He's wearing a black designer suit and holding a drink in what appears to be a goblin. I squint my eyes, thinking, *that's a little strange.*

 Brook asks me if I want to dance, but I tell her, not yet. We decide to get up and walk around. Noticing the live band playing, I start to enjoy myself. Still holding my drink and sipping it. After a few minutes I put my empty glass down on a table, when that distinguished gentleman approaches me, asking me if I'd like to dance with him. His eyes go right to my brooch. He reaches to touch it, but I back up.

Explaining, *"it was a gift, and this is incredibly special to me."*

He smiles...

 Then he says, "About that dance, shall we?"
His eyes are so hypnotizing and as dark as the evening sky.
He puts his palm out for me to take it, I can't resist him.
I don't usually dance with strangers, but this guy is spectacular.

 Leading us onto the dance floor. A moderate but slow song begins to play. Cherish the Day.

Donna Tischner

 He sways us, back and forth, in rhythm and time. His captivating persona has me in awe. He begins to talk to me as we dance, asking me my name. I speak, "Jewel." Then he says, "You're enchanting." I look at him and smile.

Putting my cheek to his chest. He rubs his hand down my back and then up. Staring at me the whole time.

He swirls me around, under his arm flawlessly, and I end up back in his arms.
His grip speaks to me, saying how he's enjoying the dance.
His hands tightened to my hips, and I feel myself growing incapacitated. I don't want to leave his arms.
He dips me back, then gently kisses my cheek. Bringing me back up.

As the dance comes to an end, and we part, I bow my head to him, and I thank him for the saccharine dance, then excuse myself.
Parting, he watches me walk back to my table.

 Ordering another drink, I think about him. He is exquisite. Tall, handsome, and muscular.
He smells delicious and is as charming as a Prince.

Kiss Of Life

Brook meets me back at our table, and she starts asking me, "Who was that guy?" I smile, saying, " I have no idea, but holy shit, he is fascinating." We laugh.

Soon the night turns into the morning, and we head back to Brook's place. Falling asleep, I begin to dream of that man I shared the dance with last night.

It's like he wants me...
I see fog in the dark hours.
He's standing in it, wearing a long black cloak.
His eyes are mesmerizing with a sparkle in them.
He stands with his hand out, calling me to come to him.

Turning and pulling the blankets,

I hear him call my name, Jewel!

I sit up in my bed, then leave the room.
Following his voice, I go outside to him.
He's standing in the fog waiting for me.
He takes my hand in his, and then picks me up in his arms, carrying me. He puts me down on a Large Basalt Flat Stone. Then kisses me. I hold him as he begins to kiss down my neck. Over my breasts.
The wind is cold, and the fog is eerie, but I feel so safe with

him. He tells me again, "you're sensational."

I jump up! My heart is pounding through my chest! Brook hears me. My breathing is labored, asking me what's wrong. I tell her I had a weird dream.

Telling Brook about the dream, I'm upset by this. She holds me, saying, "it was just a dream. You're okay now." "Yes, but it felt so real."

Brook and I talk for a while more, eat, then I leave to go home.

When I get home, there's another package at my front door. I bend down and pick it up, heading into the house. Feeling uneasy about another surprise gift, I put the box down, staring at it, wondering who keeps sending me gifts and why.

I go on about my day, trying to forget about the package. I put my Alexa on and begin singing to the tunes. I grab a few boxes and begin to pack up some of my parent's belongings. Thinking it's time to let some of their stuff go. I empty the bookshelves in the living room and stumble upon a key buried under some papers. I pick it up, wondering what it goes to; I take it and put it on the

Kiss Of Life

coffee table. After wiping the shelves clean and moving the boxes to the back of the house, I decided to look out the window. And sure enough, that man from the Victorian is looking out his window too. I move back quickly and sit on the couch.

I start to feel a little ill. Like I'm nauseous. Unsure why I feel sick, I get a glass of water. I sip it, taking the glass back to my bedroom with me, and lay on my bed. Falling asleep.

I begin to dream...

Fire, there are tall flames, blowing in the dark field, then I see him. He's walking in the fire towards me.
Calling, "Jewel! come to me." I see myself walking towards him; he puts his hand out to me, "come."
He spoke. His hand is just inches from mine. I put my hand out to him, and he takes it in his, holding on to it. He walks ahead of me pulling me, the flames are all around us.
He lays me down in the field, getting on top of me, he rubs his long nail over my lips. Then he leans in to kiss me. I kiss him back, feeling his strength and power. He tells me,
"I need to have you!"

I wake up. Breathing heavy. Scared. Troubled.

Donna Tischner

I start to feel worried, thinking about these nightmares, wondering, why am I dreaming like this? I sit there on my bed, holding my pillow.
I lay back down and fall asleep. When I awake, I'm so relieved I didn't have another dream.

Again, I hear banging sounds in the house. Jumping back, I hit my dresser, thinking, "What the hell is that?" Then the sound stops.

Two days before the block party, I decided to go pick some things up at the store. I grab my shoes and coat and head out the door. It's dark, but early yet, so I drive to the corner store, double park, by the curb, and get out of my truck, closing the door.

When I turn, I see his face! The man in my nightmares. I stumble backwards and fall, landing on my rear, scraping my hands on the cement pavement.
I push myself up, but he's gone. I turn my head both ways, looking for him. But he's nowhere in sight.

I run into the store, looking in there for him. But I don't see him. I grab what I need and get out of there, rushing home.

Kiss Of Life

I pull into my driveway, but now I'm afraid to get out of the Jeep. I look out the windows, making sure it's safe, get my house key ready, grab the bags from the store, and rush into the house.

While I'm running, one of the bags rips, and food falls out on the damp ground. Shaking my head, feeling ridiculous, I put the key in the door and open it. I put one bag down and go back outside to grab the things on the ground.

As I kneel, picking everything up, I see men's shoes next to me. I fall back. Scared to death, I look up at the man. He says, "My Master would like you to join him for drinks this evening." I stand to my feet and begin speaking to this man in a hostile voice.

"You can't just creep up on people, and I can't have drinks with your master! and why do you call him Master? That's ridiculous!"

He responds saying, " I beg your forgiveness, he's called Master because he is my employer. I will let him know you declined again."

I'm so frustrated I tell him to tell his Master whatever he likes, and I walk away, going into my house.

Donna Tischner

A few minutes later, I feel the earth shake like an Earthquake. I grab the doorjamb holding it tightly, and then fall to the floor, pictures fall off the walls, and glasses vibrate off the table, breaking. I sit there for a minute, asking myself, *did we just have an earthquake? NY doesn't usually get them.*

After I clean up the broken glass and hang the pictures back on the wall, I walk down the dark hallway to my bedroom.

As I am walking, I see him, the man I danced with, standing at the end of the hall. His face, a ghostly image on my wall, he is angry, with his pointed eyebrows and lips a thin line.

I scream and run back to the living room. Shaking, I pick up my phone and hold it thinking of calling Brook. I start to cry. Feeling scared, I sit on the couch, bringing my knees to my chin and squeezing my cell phone in my hand. I fall asleep. When I wake, I call Brook. Asking her if she felt it too last night. She asks me what I am talking about, I tell her the earthquake, and she starts to laugh! I ask her why she's laughing, still giggling. She tells me we didn't have an earthquake.

Kiss Of Life

I tell her, "Yes, we did, my pictures fell off the wall and glasses broke, of course we did!" but she swears, they didn't feel it.

We hang up. Now I'm convinced something is going on, and someone wants me. But who and what?

Finally, it's the weekend and we're setting up for the block party. The weather is gorgeous, 75 degrees, and clear sunny skies.

I take the liquor I bought and put it out on the table: some desserts and potato chips. I watch as neighbors move their cars to the end of the road blocking any cars from coming in. Others set up more tables and games.

Then Mr. Michaels strolls over to me, I ask him if he felt the earthquake too from the other night, but he looks at me like I'm crazy. He says to me, "Are you serious?" I smile at him and answer, saying, "Yes, my whole house shook, pictures fell off the walls, and glasses broke." He stands there looking at me but believes me that something did happen on my property.

I open a bottle of wine and pour myself some, downing it. I'm feeling a little overwhelmed.

Donna Tischner

Then the music starts to play loudly. I hear kids singing and parents yelling let's start the barbeque. Laughing at myself and wishing my parents were here for this.

I peek over at the Victorian, only this time, there's no one standing in the window.

When I hear a woman's, voice yell out my name, only to learn it's Brook. I run over to her hugging her. Telling Brook, I don't want to be alone at night anymore. Weird things have been happening. I don't like it.

As the sun sets and neighbors make a barn fire, we sit around it in the street, roasting marshmallow's, talking, and singing, enjoying ourselves. I look up at the Victorian, and sure enough, he's watching.

I stand, holding my wine glass up to him as if saying, *Cheers,* then take a sip. The curtains drop. I smile. Then it happens.

Kiss Of Life

Chapter 3:
DESIRE

As the night begins to fall, sitting around the fire, after giving cheers to my Victorian neighbor, I think I made him angry. Because now I see his porch light go on, and a man steps out of the front door.

He walks to the end of the long driveway and stands there. I feel a flutter in my stomach. I decide to get up and walk over to him.

I grab a bottle of wine and an extra glass. He stands with his hand on the Iron fence, watching me.

It's so dark on the corner of his property.
I can't even make out his face. I'm extremely nervous.

My dress is blowing in the wind, and my heels clatter on the pavement as I walk. I'm getting closer to him now and feeling shy, but I continue non the less.

I approach him saying, "Good evening Sir, can I offer you

some wine?"

He doesn't respond. Then I introduce myself to him. "My name is Jewel Sommers." Still no reply from him.

I pour him a glass of wine, handing it to him. But he doesn't take it. I'm baffled and a little embarrassed by his resistance. I say to him, "You don't have to be rude. I came over here to introduce myself to you and offer you some wine."
I put the wine bottle and glass on the pavement and walk away.

Then I hear him say in a low voice, "Don't go." I stop in my tracks and turn around to him. Then say,

"Now you want me to come back. You just treated me rudely!" He steps out from behind the gate and picks up the glass of wine, holds it up to me as if saying, "*Cheers,*" then drinks all of it.

I watch him from a distance. Then he says, "Come back." I do. I ask him his name. Then he says, "Romanian Vlad." I put my hand out to shake his, but he takes my hand, holding my fingers, and brings it to his lips, kissing the top of my hand, saying, "It's a pleasure to meet you

Kiss Of Life

finally." I stare at him then smile.

Then for some reason, I get a familiar scent. It's his cologne. I recognize that fragrance. It takes me back to the club, dancing. That man.

I request if he'd like to sit on the curb with me, and he does. I still can't see his face. It's too dark here, so I ask him to join us near the fire. But he tells me, "Not tonight, maybe next time." His voice is calming, and his mannerism gentle. It's like he's hypnotizing me with his presence.

He picks up my hand again, holding it with both his hands. I feel tingling inside me. My body craves him. And I don't know why.

I stand to my feet, immediately separating us, then tell him I need to get back to my friends. He stands, releasing my hand. He then asks me, "Have dinner with me this week." I tell him, "sure." I thank him for having a drink with me and leave to be with my friends. He watches me walking back to them. Then he's gone like Houdini.

At the end of the night, we clean up and go home. Brook stays with me for a little while and then drives home. We are now nearing midnight. I get under the

blankets to go to sleep. Thinking about Romanian, I drift off.
I'm not sure, but I think I'm dreaming.

I feel hands rubbing up my legs. Hot breath against my neck. I see Romanian's face. His dark eyes drift on my throat as his long black hair falls on my face. I feel a prick on my neck. Then feeling his mouth drift down to my breast. I think I moaned. Enjoying him. I feel his finger slip inside me. His bodyweight on top of me.

Twisting and moaning in my slumber. I jumped, waking up. My heart is beating so fast.

I run and turn the lights on. Look in the room for Romanian, but I don't see anyone. Look in the mirror. I put my hand to my neck, wiping it. It feels wet. I move my hair away to look harder at my throat. Feeling uneasy, I rush into the shower, cleaning myself, thinking, *what happen? Did something happen? Was that a dream? It felt too real. Why was my neck wet?*

I go back into my bedroom and get on my bed. Covering myself with the blankets. I leave the lights on to feel safer. Then I feel this sudden urge to call his name out loud. I say it, "Romanian!" I sit there, wondering what is

Kiss Of Life

going on. I put my head down on my pillow. Then drift off.

In the morning, I get out of bed, and the first thing I see is a black Rose on the floor. I bend down and pick it up. I smell his cologne. Romanian's. Now I'm convinced I wasn't dreaming last night.

I sit in my kitchen sipping a cup of coffee, wondering, and thinking about last night. I feel the need to talk to someone. Is it all the trauma from losing my dad? Am I going crazy? What do I do? A billion things are running through my mind.

By 2 o'clock I decide to go knock on Romanian's door. As nervous as I am, I still do. I approach his gate, open it, and go inside. Walk down the long walkway and up a few steps. As I near the front door, it opens. That man asks me to enter. I ask him his name, and he says, "Belvedere." He asks me, "Can I help you?" I ask to speak to Romanian. He tells me he is sleeping. I look around the house, noticing everything.

I'm standing in a vast foyer. There's a black candle chandelier hanging over my head, Red drapes hang in the doorways, and eerie pictures of older centuries hang on the walls. I feel like I just stepped into a scary movie.

Donna Tischner

I ask Belvedere to let Romanian know I stopped in to see him and that it is urgent that I speak with him today. I turn and leave his house.

Once back home, I grab that other package from a few days ago and open it. I take it out of the box. It's a Silver Jewelry set. Matching Necklace, and earring set of Rubies. Red like blood. I go to a mirror and hold the earrings up to my ear. Then put it back into the box.

It's now 5 p.m., and there's a knock at my door. I open it, seeing Belvedere. He asks me to come back to the house to see Romanian. I do. Once there, he leads me into a dark room. When he puts the lights on, they are red. I see a colossal throne chair.

Belvedere walks out, closing the door.

I stand there waiting. But I'm not alone in the room. Romanian rushes over to me. Saying,
"I'm glad you came here this evening." I ask, "Why?" "because I wanted to see you." "Why?" He smiles at me and walks away. Asking me to sit next to him on the Black Tuft Sofa.

I walk over to him, standing in front of the sofa where he

Kiss Of Life

is already sitting, and he puts his hands on my waist. I allow this because he turns me on immensely.

Then he pulls me closer to him, stands, and begins to kiss me so passionately I can't let go. When he releases me, I ask him, " What is it about you? you're so enigmatic, and my desire is increasing immensely for you." Smiling, he replies,

" I'm going to make you mine."

I laugh, saying, "How do you plan to do that?" He takes my hand, leading me into an expansive dining room. The table setting is for two with Candles that grace the long dining set. Goblins at the china side: red wine and all kinds of food on the buffet.

I look at Romanian asking, " What is this?" "You promised to have dinner with me this week."

I heard him talk in another language saying, "Printesa mea." I smiled at him not asking what he just said.

Then he says, "please call me Roman." Smiling, he pulls the tall red velvet chair out for me, and I take my seat. He sits at the head of the table, and me next to him.
 The servers come out, pouring me some wine, and asking

if I'd like the steak, asparagus, and mashed potatoes? I nod my head yes to her.

I pick up the napkin and place it on my lap. I tell Roman, "I wish I were more prepared for this. I would have dressed for the occasion." A half-smile forms at his lips, and he says, " Your black dress is more than appropriate."

I begin to eat. Roman watches me as I put the meat to my mouth, then sip my wine. He asks,

"Do you approve of this?" "Yes."

Then he begins to eat.

After we eat, the servers bring out desserts. More wine, but I pass on the dessert. Taking my wine, I stand, sip it, then tell Roman, " This is quite a house you have here. Everything is so antiquated." "Do you not approve?" Shaking my head, answering, "Oh, it's beautiful!" He takes my hand and leads me into another room.

The Parlor. He stands in front of me, his breath right on my lips. He bends down to kiss me. I feel his hand on my back. Then he puts his fingers on my breasts, sliding under

Kiss Of Life

the top of my dress.

I back up. He says, " Too soon?"

" Yes, I'm afraid it is."
"My apologies."

I stare at him, realizing he's the man I danced with at the club that night. I say to Roman,

"We shared a dance, didn't we?"
"Yes, we did."
"Can I ask you something Roman?"
"Sure."

"This is going to sound really strange. But I need to know. I feel stupid even asking this,

Were you at my house last night?"

He smiles, pondering my question, then he responds.
"I was."

"You were in my house? how'd you get in?"
"That's not important."
"But it is. Did you leave the black rose too?"
"Yes."

Donna Tischner

"Oh my God, then I wasn't dreaming?"
He doesn't reply...

Feeling a little perturbed, I tell him I must go, but he grabs my arm, pulling me into a kiss with him. I try to get out of his grip, but I can't. He holds me there, kissing me. I feel as if I'm going to pass out, from what I just heard. I place my hands on his pecks, pushing him back, but still, he doesn't let me go.

He whispers in my ear,
"I want you!" Kissing me and grabbing my face with his hand.
"Roman," I try to speak, "let me go."
"Why? I know you want me."
"Not like this! I want to go home!"
He lets me go, and I walk to the front door. Then he speaks -
"I will see you again soon!"
I turn to him, saying,
"Those packages that were left at my doorstep, were they from you too?
"Yes."
"You're the mystery man? why do you send me these gifts?"

Kiss Of Life

"I want you to have them."
"I cannot accept them. I'm giving them back to you!"

"I don't want them back, don't make me upset!"

Roman grabs me by my waist side, pushes me against the door, and kisses me. In the heated moment, he pulls my hair back and goes for my throat, sucking on it. His grind presses against me, he growls, and I shove him back. Yelling to let me leave. He opens the front door, and I walk out, not looking back, going straight home.

By the next morning, my cell rings, and it's the school Congratulating me on my new position as the Head Music Instructor and asking me to start next week.
Feeling astatic, I decide to brush up on my piano playing.

I go into the back room of the house and open all the blinds,
I sit at my father's baby grand piano and began to play. Feeling confidant, I sing and play for a few hours.

After dinner, I go to my bedroom and lay my head on my pillow, thinking of Roman. I feel my eyes getting heavy, and they close.

Donna Tischner

I see his face. He's angry. I turn to get away from him, but he grabs me. Scratching me, blood seeps to the surface of the scrape.
Ripping off my blouse. I cover myself with my arms, but he pulls my hands away, exposing my bra. I scream to him, "Roman please stop!"
But he pulls me into his arms, kissing me. "I need to have you!" he spoke, tearing off my skirt.

I try again to cover my body with my arms and hands, but he grabs them telling me not to cover myself.

I run for the door. He gets angry and grabs me by my hair. I stand there, half-naked. I feel as if I can no longer fight him, so I give in. Relaxing my arms. He takes off my bra. Picking me up and carries me to his bedroom, telling me, "this room is off-limits to everyone but you!"

I wake up! I'm soaking wet and naked. I look at the clock, the time reads, 3 a.m.

I throw on my long white nightgown and silk bathrobe. Grab my slippers and open my front door.
He's standing at his window. I close my front door and go to Roman's house.

Kiss Of Life

He watches me. All the doors open automatically. I walk into the Victorian, and Roman greets me taking my hand in his, and wrapping his arms around me to kiss me.

He lifts me in his arms and carries me to his bedroom. Lays me on his bed. Slipping the robe off my shoulders. His eyes are hypnotizing, and I melt in his arms. He brushes his fingers down my cheek.

Then he grabs me over my waist, and my arms fall back. He puts his lips to my neck. I feel a pinch. And I grab his back, digging my nails into him. As his tongue licks my throat, and back to my mouth, both sweetly and tenderly. He puts me down and glides on top of me. His hips meet mine, and he moans lustily. Then bending down and kisses my breast on the center. I hear his breathing getting heavier. And feel his long nails graze my belly.

I feel my body rise off the mattress, and my head dangles back. My arms go limp, but Roman holds me. In the air. I feel exhilarated by his every move. The lights flicker and I cry out his name. He kisses me, and I hold him saying, In a succulent voice. "You've bewitched me." I open my eyes and realize I can touch the ceiling with my fingers, but I brush the hair out of his face and kiss him affectionately. He moans and arches his back in his moment of passion.

Donna Tischner

Dragging his fingers down my chest, then squeezing my breast. He leans in and kisses them.

He brings us back down to the bed wrapping me in his grip and holds me until I fall asleep.

Kiss Of Life

Chapter 4:
HE'S AN ANIMAL

When I wake, Roman is holding me so tight I can't escape his grip. I reach up stretching my neck, and kiss him, and his eyes open. He pulls me closer. I squeeze my fingers in between his thighs and hold them.

Roman kisses me on my shoulder, then my neck, and before I know it, he's on top of me, holding me down. He pulls my wrists over my head holding them there.

 I stare up at him, and in his fiery passion, he shows me his fangs, and bends down, biting into my neck. I feel the blood dripping off my shoulder. He moans. Loving and savoring the taste of the extraction. He picks his head up and looks at me, telling me to kiss the blood off his lips, but I refuse, by turning my head away from him, and he grabs my cheeks, squeezing them, causing my lips to pucker, and he puts his mouth to mine. He rubs his bloody face on my cheeks and lips.

Donna Tischner

Turning my head, I try to avoid his face, I taste my own blood, it's like copper.

I tense up in pain as he holds my arms down, pinned to the bed. I squirm under him, pleading for him to release me. But I pass out.

He gets up and leaves the room. When I wake, I'm alone in bed. I see my blood on the sheets and feel a tear fall from my eyes. Thinking to myself, what have I done. "What the fuck?"

I get out of the bed and shower. I scrub myself clean. Crying out loud and saying, "He's horrible!"
Feeling like that was ruthless,
 I get out of the shower and look for my clothes, but there's a black gown lying on the bed when I step back into the bedroom.

I pick up the long fairy gown and step into it. I'm not too fond of it.

I step out of the bedroom and walk down the hall to the winding staircase. I make my way down and look for Roman when Belvidere tells me to come with him, walking into the dining room.

Kiss Of Life

Roman is already sitting at the table. When I enter, he stands. Telling me to come in and eat. I tell him, "No!" He says, "excuse me?" "I want to leave!" "Why?" "You're an animal and I want to leave right now!"

I turn and head for the front door. Roman chases after me, grabbing my arm and telling me, "you cannot leave." "What you did to me this morning is not acceptable!" He smiles, then begins to laugh. Saying, "That's why you're upset?" I'm so mad. I slap him across his face.

He starts to shake, his fist clench, Knuckle's turning white, standing there, his back bends over a little, letting out a whale of a scream, then the house trembles like an earthquake, I grab the wall for dear life.
I see vases fly off the table and silverware dart across the room. I duck down, sheltering my head with my arms.

Then everything stops. And Roman grabs me by my arm and pulls me up the stairs locking me in a room. I turn towards the door, banging on it, screaming, "Roman, please let me out of here!"

I rush over to the windows attempting to get them open, but either they are cemented or locked closed. I look for something to pick the lock on the door with, but I can't find anything.

I stroll over to the bed feeling disconsolate and cry, keeping my head down. *He's won*, I tell myself. *I'm never getting out of here.*

I look in the mirror and see the marks on my neck. Then I remembered the documents from my father's desk with the two teenagers. I realize now what those marks were on them. Asking myself, "Did Roman kill them?" I put my face in my hands, in shame and sobbing.

***

Downstairs Roman tells Belvidere, "I knew she was the one. She has what we've been searching for, all these years, and she's lived here her whole life. Now we know for sure.

That girl is going to give me the world. The world we once knew. She is special, keep your eyes on her, let no one touch her!"

***

Kiss Of Life

I get back up and go over to the door, calling for Roman, but he doesn't answer. I bang and bang on the door, making a ruckus until the door unlocks. I turn the nob and step out into the hall.

I look left and then right for anyone in the hallway, but don't see anyone, feeling like this is a trick, I walk up to another set of stairs and call, "Roman?" I see his room. I open the door. Then step in. But he's not there. I climb on his bed and lay down and close my eyes.

I kept my eyes closed for a few seconds. When I open them, I see him. Then pick my head up, Roman is sitting on the side of the bed next to me. I move away. He begins to talk, saying,

"Why are you in my room?"
"I was looking for you."
"What did you want?"
"I want to talk to you about a few things."
"What things?"
"Why didn't you tell me your secret? being a Vampire?"
"I knew you'd figure it out."
"Why'd you bite me like that this morning?"

Roman doesn't answer. Instead, he laughs amusingly. "Well, are there more of you out there?"

"Yes."
"Is there a leader?"
"Yes."
"Who?"
"I am."

I stare off for a few minutes. Looking at the floor with my fingers entwined. Then I ask one last question.

"Are you going to kill me?"

He gets reticent. Standing, he watches my expression. Then says,

"If I were going to kill you, I would have done it already. Didn't I say I was going to make you mine?"
"You can't treat me the way you did this morning. I'm not your toy."

"I can treat you any way I want!"
"Not if you want me to be with you. You will respect me!"

Kiss Of Life

"Are you giving me orders?"
"Maybe, I won't allow you to hurt me again! I can tell the police your little secret."
"There's nothing you can do about it!"

Roman gets in my face, staring heavily into my eyes, then says.
"you will never speak of this to anyone! I could take your life in a second!"
"I want to go home. Can I leave?"
"Go..."

As I stand and walk towards the bedroom door, he takes me by my hand. I look at his hand as he grabs mine, my eyes follow his body up to Romans eyes, then he says,

"You can leave, but you can never go."
I ask him in a low voice,
"Can I go to my house?"

He drops my hand and opens the door for me to leave. I walk out and run down the stairs to the front door, making my way back to my house.

As I get in, I call Brook. Crying hysterically. She tells me to *calm down*, saying, *I can't understand you*. Then she says she's coming over, but I tell her not to come. I'm worried about her safety.

I tell her about the man from the club, the one I danced with. And how we hooked up now. She begins to question me,

"That good-looking man?"
"Yes, that guy."
"What do you mean you hooked up with him? How?"
"He's my neighbor."
"Holy shit, really? so what happen?"
I begin to feel like I shouldn't tell her too much, so I change my story, thinking she could be in danger.
Feeling stupid, I tell her,
"We had a big fight over something so crazy.
Roman bought me a dress, and he wanted me to wear it, but I didn't like it and told him no!"

"So that's his name, Roman? what did the dress look like?"
"The dress is black, long, and lacey."
"Okay, you hated the dress, and you fought over that?"
"Yes. We'll make up tomorrow, I'm sure. But he upset me over it. I'm sorry to call you with this."
"Don't apologize, you know you can always tell me

Kiss Of Life

anything!"

After talking to Brook for a while longer, we hang up. I begin to feel a little better. Then decide to go back into the office a look at those documents.

I turn the light on and sit at the desk, opening the drawer and pulling out the papers. I read them. This time I read the whole document.

Two teenagers have been found dead near the East Point Lake. Cause of death, unknown. But two marks have been found on their necks.

The Coroner's report said these were not snake bites, and they are unsure what the two tiny marks can be.

The Coroner speculated, possible Bat Bite.
Blood samples were taken. Rabies virus was not found.
I search the desk for more information. I find a pad with my father's notes written on it. It reads.
No Rabies, no infectious disease, not a snake bite. Only other explanation, Vampire.

I sit there staring at his paper, realizing he knew something. That's why he ended up dying. I leave the office and go into my bedroom.

Donna Tischner

I begin to think of Roman. Then I hear banging from the other room. I jump and grab my cell, scared, I run to the front door but don't open it. The banging continues, and I run out onto the lawn standing there. I feel like there's someone in the house.

I look up at Roman's house and see him staring out the window. But I don't want to ask him for help, fearing he'll bite me, or lock me in the room again if I end up back at his house.

I go back into my house and listen.
Standing still, I wait. But I don't hear anything.
I walk over and sit on the sofa. Holding my phone and biting my nails.
Then I hear the banging again. I jump off the couch and stand near the front door, waiting to run out. My heart is pounding out of my chest.

It gets louder. I think the sound is coming from my parent's bedroom. I haven't been in there, not once. It was over five years ago the last time I stepped into their bedroom.

I start to think, maybe it's an animal, or perhaps the

Kiss Of Life

window broke, maybe the window is open, and something is blowing around. I walk down the long dark hallway to their room and put my ear to the door, listening for any sound. Then it starts again, banging and thrashing like something is trying to get out.

Grabbing my keys, I run to the front door. Fumbling to put the key in the keyhole of my truck, shaking uncontrollably, I managed to get it in.

I sit, then starting the truck, my knees bouncing up and down, heading towards Brook's house.

As I drive to my corner, Roman is standing in the middle of the street, with his hands on his hips, his legs spread apart, and a look in his eyes that can paralyze you. The wind is blowing his long dark hair back, and I slam on my brakes.

I sit behind the wheel, watching him. Shaking, I know I'm in trouble. "Fuck!"

He spoke no words. I put the truck in reverse and back it into my driveway. Sitting there. Looking at him. He stands at my door and says to me, "Get out!" I open the door and step out. Then Roman asks me, 'Where were you going?" "That's none of your business!" I see the look in his eyes, blood-red and fire. I guess I pissed him off. He grabs my wrist, pulling me towards his house. I tell him, "No! I won't go back there. You'll only lock me up again!" Roman stands there in the street, looking at me.

Shaking my head back and forth, pulling my wrist from his grip, I begin telling him, " I think someone is in my house!"

He pulls me by my arm, and we enter my house. I don't even need to say another word; he walks right to my parent's bedroom; his head turns quickly to the closet.

He tries to open the door but says,
"It's locked." The banging persists, only more intensely now. I move to the hallway, fearful. Then I remembered the key I found. I run and grab it. I'm trembling, handing it over to Roman.

He slips the key in and turns the doorknob. To my surprise, there is a Vampire bound by silver chains and gagged. Roman picks him up. Then he looks at me and tells me to move away, fearing this vampire will try to attack me. He removes the gag, asking what happen. But the other vampire doesn't answer. Roman takes him, practically flies him to his house to take care of him.

Kiss Of Life

I'm left standing in my parent's room, unsure what the hell just transpired. Minutes later, Roman comes back and grabs me, gliding me back to his house.
I'm now being placed on his bed. Roman tells me to change into the garment on his bed. I look over at it and see a red silk nightgown.

I change into it. Then sit on his bed. Looking up at the four-posted canopy, with heavy black drapes dangling to the floor.

Waiting, I climb up to the pillows putting my head down and falling asleep. It's been hours since Roman left me here.

Soon I awaken to hands rubbing up my legs. Roman begins to kiss my thighs, working his way to my lips. Telling me how much he wants me. Kissing me more, over my neck. He grabs my waist, lifting me a little, and proceeding to kiss my mouth. He lines my lips with his tongue; then I feel it slip in. I start to feel enticed by him. Moaning, I place my hands on his shoulders. He becomes feisty in his elation, he bends down, and his fangs sink into my neck. Gently he begins to suck, leaving the area clean.

He lies me back down on the pillows and climbs on top of

me, swaying his hips and grabbing my back. His tongue drags over my breast. I wrap my arms around his neck, holding him and rubbing his back. He then pushes up a little, still connected to me, and he stares down at my body, his nails drag down my abdomen back to my neck. He pushes my hair back and bites me on the other side of my throat. There is no pain.

Feeling his manhood moving, Roman squeezes me in his jubilation and lays me down. Finishing, he holds me close to him.

We sleep till mid-afternoon the next day. When I wake, Roman is dressing, telling me to meet him in the dining room.
Before he leaves the room, he walks over to me in bed, leans down, kisses me softly, and then drags his fingers over my cheek. I hold his hand and then sit up, pulling him in for a deeper kiss. He smiles and tells me not to take too long.
I shower and then find clean clothes on the bed for me. I pick up the long black skirt and puff white shirt and put them on, heading downstairs.

I walk into the dining room, Nocturnes, Op. 9: By Chopin, is playing softly in the background. It's a beautiful piano

Kiss Of Life

piece.

Roman stands to pull my chair out. The servants begin to pile food onto my plate. I place my napkin on my lap and sit there. Roman notices I haven't touched my food and asks,
"Something on your mind?"
I smile and pick up my fork, playing with my lunch. Again, he asks, "Something on your mind?" I ask him.

"Why do you want me here with you? It's not like you're in love with me. It's not like you can't have whomever you want. You're a rich, good-looking, and powerful man who can have anyone, so why me?"

Roman says, "You're wrong."

I tilt my head, saying,
"Wrong about what?
I think you've been very surreptitious."
A smile grazes his face. He puts his hand on my arm,
tilting his head, then says,
"I want you here, isn't that enough?"
"No, I want more."
"More? Jewelry? Money?"
"No... None of that... You, your love."

Donna Tischner

Roman stands and walks over to me, and kisses the top of my head, walking out of the room.
I start feeling, my heart is heavy, what is it that he wants from me?

***

Roman speaks with Belvidere saying, "Her beauty is enchanting, and she is making me feel uncertain of things." Belvidere replies to Romanian saying,

"Uncertain Sir?"
"Yes, I want her to be with me all the time now, but Jewel wants more."
"More Sir?"

"Yes, my love. It has been far too long since I have loved any woman."
"Maybe your questioning, do you love her? I think you do Sir."

Kiss Of Life

Chapter 5:
FALLING

I secretly follow Roman to where he is going. He walks down to a cellar. It looks more like a dungeon: cement floor and sconces with flames burn on the cement walls.

Walking down the long hall, I stay close to the wall. Leading me to a room where the other Vampire is.

 I hear cries coming from a man, the door is ajar. I peek through the crack. Right away, I'm spotted.

Roman is accosted, asking what I am doing down here. He pulls me into the room with the sick vampire. He's chained to the bed, with blood flowing in his I'V. Roman holds my wrist tightly, I pull, but he won't let go.

Then he tells me who the man is. "Jeremy Thyme." Explaining, my father had caught him and chained him like an animal. Locking him in his closet for over 5 weeks. I gasp.

 Putting my hand to my mouth. Then apologize to him. Roman tells me he's over 100 years old. But he looks like he's 20. Long brown hair and hard features, with his blue eyes. Exceptionally good looking.

Roman tells me, " your father found out about us from the marks on those teenagers and set up a trap catching Jeremy. He was bitten after he locked Jeremy up. Another vampire wanted to know where Jeremy was, but your father wouldn't tell him. The one that bit him, fixed it so no marks would be visible.

I begin to cry so much Roman has to carry me out of the cellar bringing me upstairs. I was shocked when he held me in his arms for a few minutes, telling me he is sorry. Then kisses me. I look up at him wiping my eyes; I tell him, "Thank you."

He pours me a glass of Chateau Lafite Rothschild.
I sip the expensive wine and ask him, "Now what? what are you going to do with me?" Roman again doesn't answer. As we sit on the sofa, he picks me up, putting me on his lap. Holding me there, he kisses me. I put my head on his shoulder, and he rubs my hair. I'm wondering what is going on here and why he is being so attentive to me. Leaving it alone, I let Roman continue to hold me.

As we loll on the sofa, he tells me, "You are precious to

Kiss Of Life

me, and I can't lose you." I lift my head looking at him, then lay it back down.

Later he releases Jeremy and tells me he will be joining us for dinner. I make no comment. Roman assures me he cannot touch me. He has to obey him.

I change for dinner, putting on whatever was left out for me. This time it's a red form-fitting gown off the shoulders. Next to the gown is a Ruby diamond neckless. I put it on and go into the dining room.

When I step into the dining room, both gentlemen stand.

Roman greets me with a peck to my cheek, pushing in my chair. We sit.

Jeremy stares at me, making me feel uncomfortable and Roman looks at him; his eyes tell Jeremy to stop staring. I begin to think, "What is Roman going to do with Jeremy?" then Roman speaks, saying, "Jeremy will be staying here for a little while longer." I'm thinking to myself, "This is going to be bad, with him here. I don't trust Jeremy."

Roman's eye squint, causing his eyebrows to meet in the middle as if he knows exactly what I'm thinking.

Donna Tischner

Then he says, "Jeremy will not be around you ever! except when we are together to eat!"

 I play with my food then take a bite. I ask Roman with my mind, "Can you hear my thoughts?" Roman smiles at me then sips his drink. I decide to play a little game to see for myself if he can read my mind.

So, I think, "This needs salt."
keeping my head down. Then the salt is placed by my plate. I look up at Roman. And say, "thank you."
Then Roman says to me, "I don't like games." I just give him a look and continue to eat.

Sometime later, we retrieve to the living room, and I sit on the sofa. Roman comes in and tells me how Radiant I look this evening. Smiling, I say, " Your kind."

I leave the room, excusing myself for a moment, and Jeremy walks in. He pours himself a drink. I hear them talking. Jeremy asks Roman, "Does she know?" Roman tells him, "No." Then Jeremy says, "It's her blood, isn't it?" Roman hurries to his side, grabbing him by the throat and telling him, "If you ever touch her, I'll kill you! You're not to be near her!" Roman releases him, and they separate to different parts of the room. When I walk back in, I feel

Kiss Of Life

the tension.

Asking, "Is everything okay?" Jeremy leaves.

Roman asks me to sit next to him. I walk over and sit, holding his hand.

He wraps his arm around my shoulder, forcing my head on his chest. I ask him, "Why are you acting like you love me all of a sudden?" He doesn't answer. Instead, he kisses me and keeps on kissing me until I feel him on top of my body. Moving his hands to my breasts and kissing my neck. I try to push him off me, asking him not to bite me again. Parting, he says, " If I wasn't falling, I would not respect your wishes." I look at him, unsure what that means. I don't question it.

I begin to feel tired and tell Roman I'm going to sleep. I walk up the stairs to my room and change, getting under the blankets, thinking, "He can read my mind. What else isn't he telling me?" I close my eyes and drift off. I don't see Roman for the next day.
When I return to the dining room, I ask Belvedere, "Where is Roman?" He tells me, "he's out on business." Then I ask him, "Can I leave to go to my house?" but he tells me, "I don't think that's a good idea." I tell Belvedere,

Donna Tischner

"I need to go home. I have to prepare for my new job," I open the door and walk out, crossing the street to my house.

I walk into my living room and look around. Then shower, changing my clothes into something more normal. When I'm done, I go into my parent's room and sit on their bed... Some time passes, and I get up, leaving their room. I feel lost without Roman. I don't know why. But I miss him.

Then there's a knock at my door. I attempt to answer but, I look to see who it is before opening. I see its Jeremy. I'm afraid to open the door. So, I pretend no one's home. But he says, "I know you're there. I can smell you through the doors." I ask him,
"What do you want?" but he just says,
"Open the door!"

"No, Roman said we're not to be alone in the room. He should be present."
"Just open the door."

I start to meditate, calling Roman to come. I send him telepathic messages of me being in trouble. I don't even know if Roman is getting my signs. But I continue calling him.

Kiss Of Life

Jeremy begins to fuss with the doorknob, turning it. Saying,

"Open the door now!"

Then I hear him kick the door with his shoe.
I say to him,
 "Just tell me what you want first."
Stalling him, I ask again,
 "What do you want?"

Jeremy gets mad and kicks the door down; I back up, falling backward on the carpet. He gets in my face, telling me,
 "Your blood is vital, and I need some now!!"

He leans over me, but a strong force is pulling him off me and Jeremy is thrown into a wall. I look and see it's Roman.

He's so irate he begins throwing him around like a rag doll! My heart is pounding so fast I feel like I'm going to have a heart attack! Roman then takes him, "I'm going to finish you now!" But Jeremy begs for his life. Roman glides him out of the house to a wooded area, asking him, "What did you tell her?" "I told her the truth! That it's her

Donna Tischner

blood you want!"

Roman throws Jeremy into a tree. He lays on the ground looking up at Roman, his hands blocking his face.

Roman yells to him,
"Why? Why would you tell her that?"
"Because she should know!"

Again, Roman picks him up slamming him into the tree grabbing his throat.
 Then saying,
"That wasn't your place to tell her!"

Roman then exiles Jeremy, telling him, "Never show your face here again!"

 Then he comes back for me, taking me back to his house.

Questioning, why didn't I just stay in the bedroom? I try to explain I have a job to prepare for, and I needed to get home. But Roman tells me, "There will be no job! you will be staying with me from now on." I start to cry.

Roman stands in front of me, placing his hand to my chin, and lifting it, for me to look him in his eyes; I stare, he

Kiss Of Life

bends down and kisses me. But I question him again, "Why am I here with you? Why do you want me here? is it my blood?"

He takes his index finger, waving it back and forth in front of my face, as if telling me, not to ask that again.

"Then just tell me, why am I here? What is it you want from me? Jeremy said my blood was vital; what did he mean?"

"Forget him! You're mine now, and no one will ever touch you again!"

I watch as Roman sits on the bed, I walk over and straddle him, he holds me, and I kiss him. I can't help myself; I tell him, "I love you Roman. If it's my blood you want, you can have it because I don't want to live without you."

Roman stands with me still on his lap and lays me gently on his bed. I see a different look in his eyes; it's not a fearful one, but tender. I reach up and kiss him, telling him, "I want you."

I feel his body growing in his leather pants, as his fingers graze my lips. He bites me over my breast, I feel the sting and let out a cry, then kisses my lips, I taste my own blood. He bites me again, then tells me, "This is the kiss of life. Soon I will make you like me." And we'll be together forever."

I rub his face, pushing the hair behind his ears, kissing him. My feelings for him have grown into something unthinkable.

I cannot deny him anymore; my love is growing stronger. I know he knows I'm not lying because he can read my mind.

Then he leans into me and says, "I'm falling for you."

I begin to feel a sense of relief. "Roman, I will wait infinitely for your love."

Kiss Of Life

Chapter 6:
FIGHT OR FLIGHT

At dinner, Roman tells me we are departing for Romania in a few days. I practically choke on my food, coughing and then picking up my water, sipping it. Then I ask him.

"What do you mean leaving for Romania?"
"I have business there, and I want you with me."
Sipping my water some more, I shake my head, informing him,

"I can't go! Romania? Seriously? No!"
"You will speak no more of this! You're going! that's final!"
"Just once, can't you wait till after dinner to spring bad news on me? I never finish a meal!"

I stand, sliding my chair out, and throw my napkin on my plate, walking away. I run up the stairs to my room and slam the door.

When Belvidere walks in, asking if he should bring me back down. Roman tells him, "No, just let her be."

Donna Tischner

Roman tells Belvidere to bring me up a fresh dinner plate and a glass of wine. When Belvidere knocks, I don't respond to him. He places my dish out in the hallway on the floor. I don't touch the food.

Later, Roman goes to his room; I can feel him reading my thoughts. My head starts to pound, and I get nauseated. I sit on my bed, telling him mentally to stop. I put on some music to try and drown him out of my mind. It seems to be working.

I open the closet and start looking at all the pretty new gowns, moving the clothes to one side as I linger through them. I spot something; it looks like a door.
I put my ear to it, listening for anything. But I hear nothing.

I lift the small lever and push the door. I see steps. I go up to them—another door. I turn the knob and walk into the room. Roman is standing there with his arms folded and a look on his face of anger. I slam the door shut and run back down. Laughing. Then I close the closet door standing in front of it, blocking it with my back. Roman pushes the door, and I stumble across the room. I smile at him. Then let out a laugh. He's not amused. Standing

Kiss Of Life

again with his arms folded and that look on his face. I roll my eyes, and he says to me,

"What were you doing?"
"Nothing, I saw a door and wanted to know where it led to, that's all."
"Why are you so curious?"

I shrug my shoulder.
"Meet me in my room in one hour!"
Roman said, walking out of the room.

I shower and get ready to go to sleep, sitting on my bed and closing my eyes. Over an hour passes, and Roman is angry. The house shakes, and I wake holding onto my bedpost.

Then my door flies open, slamming into the wall, and Roman yells,
"Why are you so DEFIANT?"

I feel my eyes get big, opening wide.
This is it; I think to myself, Flight or Fight.

"You can't keep ordering me around! Maybe you should try asking me next time!"

Donna Tischner

"There is no asking! When I say to be somewhere, you are to be there!"

"No! it doesn't work that way, I'm afraid!"

Roman is so deranged he grabs me by my throat, lifting me off the floor, slamming me into the wall, shouting. "You will obey me!"

I cannot speak. My eyes tear up. I grab his hand with mine, trying to pull them off from me. He puts me down. Pointing his finger at me and yelling,

"There won't be a next time!" I say with my mind to him, "What is your fucking problem!" He glides quickly over to me, again seizing my neck strangling me. I reach my arms around to hold him, trying to hug him. I tell him with my mind, "I love you!" He carries me to my bed, placing me on it. Letting go of me. Then leaves the room.

In the morning, I stay in bed, not going to breakfast. I don't want to see Roman. I know he'll be angry, but I don't care.

When Roman enters the dining room, asking Belvidere, "Where is Jewel's?" Belvidere replies, "She hasn't come

Kiss Of Life

down yet."
Roman punches the table, and food vibrates off to the floor.

Belvidere says to Roman, "She's a feisty lady, she never gives up, she fights for what she believes in no madder the cost."

Roman shakes his head up and down in agreement with Belvidere. Then Roman asks him, "What am I supposed to do with her?"

"You have never let anyone get to you the way she does. You have never fought with a woman the way you fight with her. I fear she is the one. She is most loyal to you, she has a caring way, and I believe she will be most devoted. I also believe you love her more than you realize."

Roman tells Belvidere, "I am falling for her, but she is so defiant! She makes me act irrational."

Belvidere smiles, then says, "Romanian, Sir, are you sure you want to take her with you?" Roman speaks, "Why do you ask that?" "Because she is strong minded and may be of some sought of trouble, with the others, they may not be able to stay away from her." Roman agrees.

Donna Tischner

By afternoon I still haven't come out of my room, nor have I eaten a thing.

I stayed in bed, sleeping on and off.

By dinner time, I open my eyes and see Roman sitting in a chair, his foot leaning on his knee, his elbow on his thigh, and his hand holding his chin up. I pick my head up, look at him, then put it back down.

Throwing the covers over my head. Roman stands, walk's over to my bed, then pulls the blankets off me. I shove my head under my pillow, and he gets mad, grabbing the pillow and throwing it to the floor. Now yelling for me to get out of the bed.

I bring my knees up to my chin, laying on my side in bed, and begin to cry, saying to him, "please just go away! Leave me be!" Roman leans over me, sliding his hands under my body, and carries me to the shower. Making me stand, he turns it on. Coldwater rushes over my head and down my shoulders, and I yell, "Please turn it off, stop, please!"

My nightgown is stuck to my body, and I crouch down,

Kiss Of Life

putting my head on my knees and my hands over my head. He pulls me to my feet, and I stand feeling defeated. He leaves the room, telling me to be downstairs in 15 minutes.

I dress for dinner and go to the dining room. Dinner is being served when I walk in. Roman says, "You kept us waiting long enough. Now sit."
I tell Roman with my mind, "I hate you! I hate you so much!" He gives me the death stare.

After dinner, Roman tells me to leave, go back to my house, but not to disappear in my truck. I look at him in shock! Then say, "Really?" He takes my hand in his and kisses the tops of my fingers, opening the front door. I walk out and go home.

I walk into my house and go right to my bed, crying in my pillow and screaming so loud. All this animosity built up has caused me so much grief.

2 days later, still home, I haven't seen or heard from Roman, I decide to get up and go into my parent's bedroom. Looking through their things in the big walk-in closet. I pull out boxes and bags. I slide my hand on top of the door molding, looking for anything. I open my father's luggage, and there are papers and notebooks. Sitting on

the floor in their closet, I start to read them. I stumble upon one book, it's in my father's handwriting. It reads,

A vampire called "SKID." He is responsible for many deaths in this area, known for hiding in trees and dropping on his prey.

They never see him coming. They never have a chance to escape. He lands on their backs and bites them instantly. Then he takes their bodies and dumps them in a wooded area, leaving them to decompose. Or unless someone finds the body first.

I keep reading.
Skid is dark-skinned with green eyes, a medium-size build, and curly long thick hair. He usually wears black leather pants and a leather vest. A necklace made of ropes with a pendant of a sacrificial gold cross. He's quick and ruthless. He shows no mercy.

I turn the page.
I have been investigating him now for a year. Watching his every move. He lives in the next town. I believe other Vampires live there as well.
I think he killed my wife...

Kiss Of Life

I stop reading, shocked! I grab my mouth with my hand. I feel my eyes watering up, and then the flow of tears run down my cheeks so fast, I throw everything off me running to the bathroom. I feel like I'm going to vomit, and then I do.

I fall on the bathroom floor hysterically, crying.

After the shock, I go back into my parent's closet and throw everything back in the luggage, hiding it in the corner. I stay on the floor crying in the closet.

Then Roman comes in, he says, "Shish, I'm here now." He picks me up and places me on my parent's bed. I ask him, "What are you doing here?"

"I felt your pain and knew I had to come to you."
"How'd you get in?"
"That's not important."

He leaned over and kissed me, asking me what happened, when I explained, "Skid" killed my mother. He questions me about how I know who Skid is. I tell him,

"I found some documents explaining who he is."
"What documents?"
"Just something my father had."

Donna Tischner

"I want to see these papers."
"Can you just hold me, please?"

He pulls me into a tender hug, holding me, kissing the top of my head. I cry on his shoulder, and he lifts my chin, kissing me and wiping the tears from my eyes.

I move a little to see his face and tell him,

"Skid hides in the trees, then torpedoes them. Roman, he needs to be stopped."

"This is who we are."
"No, you're not like him."
"I'll talk to him."

Crying more, Roman leaves the room, bringing me back a glass of wine, telling me to sip it. I do.

Then he asks me, "About those documents, I'd like to take a look at them."

"Can it wait, please?"

"For now, but eventually, I'll want them. Now, come back with me to my house." "Okay."

Kiss Of Life

Once back at Romans, he brings me into the throne room. I stand there looking at the two huge throne chairs covered in red velvet, and Romans says, pointing at the throne, "this one is going to be yours." I don't respond.

He then takes me by my hand, leading me to his bedroom.

He dims the lights and begins to undress himself. I walk over to him and help Roman out of his shirt, kissing his chest, then unbuttoning his pants.

I rub his back and thighs, taking down his pants. Kissing his inner thighs. Roman grabs my hair, and I kiss him all over. Dragging my tongue down his leg and closing my mouth on top of him. He moans. Then grabs me, leading us over to the bed, lying down.

Roman wraps his arms around my waist, holding me, then kisses me. He puts his lips to my breast, then gently bites, sucking my blood. I hold him taut. Digging my nails into his back. Once he's on top of me, I feel him growing more inside my body. Moving up and down. I feel us leave the mattress and float to the ceiling. My head dips back, and my arms drop to the side. He holds me, moaning. "Oh god!" I cried. He pulls me to his chest, holding me and sucking on my neck, then my breasts. In his delight, we are lowered back to the mattress. And I begin to cry. Roman then says to me, "You make me crazy."

I cry more, and he puts his arms around me. Saying, "You're the only one I've ever cared about. No other has ever made me feel the way you do!"

I roll on top of him, straddling him and saying, "I'm so in love with you, I never want to be apart from you again."

Roman holds me through-out the night as we sleep. In the morning, he kisses me, asking me to come to breakfast. I tell him I'll be down shortly.

I shower and change into the purple gown, it's pretty with off-the-shoulder puff long sleeves, it leaves my cleavage showing.

I head to the dining room, and Roman greets me with a kiss to my lips, then pushes in my chair.

Belvidere greets me too, saying, "It's nice to see you this morning." I smile.

Roman and I eat. And then I sip my coffee, watching Roman. His expressions are unreadable today. He hears

Kiss Of Life

my thoughts, then smiles. I squint my eyes and tilt my head to him, asking, "What's going on?" But they say nothing to me.
Sometime later, Roman asks me about going to Romania, telling me he would like me to accompany him. I put my head down and take a deep breath. Roman holds my hand, rubbing my fingers, waiting patiently for my reply. I look up at him and say,
"I would be honored to accompany you to Romania."

He says to me, "I know you don't want to go, but I'm jovial; you said yes."
Then he tells me we will be leaving in a day.

I ask him why we are going and who will be with us, he replies, I have personal business to take care of, and many will be accompanying us. He then says to me, "you will be by my side the whole time. I ask, "should I be worried?"
"No."
Then Roman says, "Let us take a look at those documents at your father's house." I look at him, and he takes my hand, leading me out the door.

Once in my house, we go to my parent's bedroom, opening the closet, I pull out the suitcase, and Roman opens it. Looking at the documents, he says, "Your father was keeping records on us?"

Donna Tischner

I look at him, shrugging my shoulders and making my eyebrows raise.

He then finds a notebook with information on other vampires. Reading them, it said,

Romanian Vlad, the 3rd, Father Vampire, to many, maybe thousands. Still Living.
Justina Vlad, second in command until her death 100 years ago.
Cause of death, murder. Wife of Romania Vlad the 3rd.
Nuno Thomas. Vicious maneater. Still living.
Jeremy Thyme, Skid Sowers, and Ann Shoemaker, ruthless, merciless, and all still living.

Romanian now, this one is special. First in Command. Mind reader. His looks are paralyzing.
He puts a spell on you. Causing you to sleep.
You think you are dreaming. But you're not. The dream, it's real! And really happening.
It has been said, the right mortal, with the right blood, will give him more power. Power unknown to anyone.
I stand there reading this and swallow. I'm profoundly astonished. My mind drifted back to Roman, my dreams, and the dance club.

Kiss Of Life

I can't even speak. I run out of the room, and Roman chases after me, grabbing my arm. I start yelling at him, saying,
"You did this to me. You tricked me! You don't even love me. It's my blood you want! How can you do this?"
Holding my arm, he yells back at me,
"Stop! Yes, it's your blood, but I do care for you! I didn't trick you! I knew you wanted me, and I had to show you through your dreams who I am."

"No, this is a trick too. I don't trust you!"
"I will prove I care for you, you can stay here, and I will leave. But I need to take these documents with me."

"That doesn't prove anything."

I begin to cry, putting my head down. Roman holds me, saying,
"I'm sorry. What can I do to show how I feel for you?"
"Right now, I just want to be alone."
"If that's really what you want, then I will honor your wishes."
I put my head down, but Roman lifts my chin, then delicately kisses my lips. Saying to me, "Please, don't

Donna Tischner

forsake me."

I feel the tears build. I open the door, holding it for him to leave. He looks back at me and says, "I will see you soon."

Kiss Of Life

Chapter 7:
ROMANIA

A few hours pass, and I take a glass of wine to my room with me. Sitting on my bed and sipping my drink, thinking about Roman and all that has transpired. I feel trounce. I send Roman messages telepathically.

I'll always love you! And I won't forsake you! NEVER!

I begin to talk to my deceased parents, asking questions. "Did you see this coming? Why wasn't I warned? I need your help."

I leave my bedroom sitting at my father's piano, pressing the keys one by one. I realize I'm not even playing a melody, just hitting the keys. Feeling lost and alone.

I drink the rest of my wine and lay down, closing my eyes. In my slumber, I begin to dream.

I see him. Roman, he is running with me on a sandy beach. The sun is shining. It's a warm summer's day.

Donna Tischner

It's like in slow motion. He lets go of my hand and runs ahead of me. I run to him; he's laughing. As I get closer, he lifts me, spinning us around and kissing me. The sandy water splashes up on us.
He bends down and grabs some shells, handing them to me. I'm smiling, sincerely. We're happy. He leads me to sit in the sand, kissing me, he lays us down. I touch his lips with my finger, then slide my hands down his muscular torso, and he rolls us into the water. He then stands and pulls me to my feet. He gets on one knee, pulls a velvet box out of his pocket, and holds it open to me, Roman proposes.

It's sweet. Tender. Romantic. I stand, crying, telling him yes. He picks me up, kissing me.

I wake to the sun streaming through my bedroom window. When I put my feet to the floor, I'm standing in bouquets of flowers, my jaw drops. *Holy shit! Roman.*
I quickly shower and throw on a black dress. I know Roman's going to want me there with him. I grab some of the flowers from my floor and go to Romans. As I approach his door, it opens automatically. I enter. But I don't see him. I call, but no answer. Then I call Belvidere. No answer.

Kiss Of Life

I go up to Roman's room and open his door. Bouquets of flowers everywhere! I feel my mouth open, my eyes getting wider, and then I see Roman. Smiling. Holding flowers in his hands. I put the flowers down and run to him, hugging and Kissing him all over his face. Then I tell him how sorry I am and that I love him, but he puts his finger to my lips, shushing me. He lifts me up, carrying me to his bed.

Slowly he begins to undress me. Loving my lips and rubbing my bottom.

He brings my leg over his shoulder and kisses my inner thigh. His hair falls over his face, and I push it back. Slow and steady, his hands glide up to my breast. I feel goosebumps and the hair on my arms rise. Savoring this moment, he moves smoothly on top of me.

Feeling stimulated, in his spirited moment, like time had stood still, and we're lost in this moment.

He whispers in my ear, "You're beautiful, and you're mine now." I grab him, holding him tightly, and cry in his chest. He smiles at me then puts his big hand around my head, holding me, kissing me.

Today, he never bit me, never hurt me, and didn't leave

me.

After breakfast, we set off for Romania. Making our way to Romans private Jet. I look at the size of it, walking up the steps going into the plane. Roman pulls me gently, saying, "We will be in this private room." As I enter, the room on the Jet is big, with a King size bed and Grey drapes that fall off the bedposts. He tells me to make myself comfortable and leaves to talk to the pilots.

5 hours into the skies, and Roman brings me a glass of wine. Sipping my drink, we talk to the others on board.
I have met a female vampire named "Tessa." She is sweet and stunning with her long blond hair and thin tall body. She doesn't seem to mind me being a mortal at all.

Later I begin to feel tired and go into our private room to sleep for the flight duration. When Roman joins me.

He tells me, "Once we arrive in Romania, things will be somewhat different. You will have to sleep in your own private quarters. We cannot be together all the time. There will be breakfast every day with the others, and dinner too. There will be times you will have to be alone while I'm out on business. Belvidere will be your personal assistant."

Kiss Of Life

I sit up on the bed staring at him, making noises with my breath, furrowing my eyebrows, and crossing my arms, saying,

"You told me we would be together the whole time, and you wouldn't leave my side! You fucking lied to me, if I had known this, I wouldn't have gotten on this Jet."

"Romania is different, this castle belonged to my parents, and we must follow the laws of the Gods."

"You're changing your words now! This isn't what you told me days ago. I don't want to be away from you, you know this! That is so messed up!"

Roman reaches to hold me, but I pull away from him, I'm angry leaving the room and sitting with Tessa
.
Tessa asks me,
    "you and Roman fighting?" "No, we just had an argument."
    "You're fighting."
She laughs... I just look at her.

"Do you want to talk about it?"
"No, thank you."

Donna Tischner

Just then, Roman walks in, telling me to get back in the room. I give him a look, then get up, walking into the room with him. He says to me,

"I don't want you talking to anyone about us!"
"But I didn't."
"You will remain in this room for the duration of the flight!"

I shake my head back and forth, giving him the death stare, sitting on the bed. Trying not to let him into my mind, but then I slip, thinking,
"Fuck You!"
He grabs me by my throat, holding me in the air, then tosses me across the room; bleeding from my arm, he tells me,
"get that cleaned up before they smell it!"
I told him to fuck off.

I walk into our private bathroom and wipe the blood, bandaging it up, then go back and sit on the club chair near the bed. As Roman is leaving the room, I gave him the finger.

As Roman demanded, I remain in the room; sitting on the

Kiss Of Life

chair, I start to cry, keeping my face down and my hands on my head.

I get so frustrated, I stand, walking to the door, and kick it with my foot, repeatedly kicking it and yelling at him, screaming,
 "Why are you so fucked up? Why do you have to be so hurtful? I want to go home!"

The others on the Jet look at Roman with heightened eyebrows and smiles of laughter. Roman shakes his head back and forth and enters the chambers. He grabs my arm, lifting me slightly off the ground, asking if I'm going to be this much trouble in Romania? I don't respond to him, and he gets furious. Yelling at me to answer, I shrug my shoulder. He tells me to look him in the eye, but I won't. He forces me to pick my head up and look at him; when I do, he tries to kiss me, but I turn my head. Telling him with my mind,
  "Go away! Right now, I really hate you!"
He puts me down then leaves again.

Roman speaks with the other vampires on the Jet, some of them saying to him,
 "You have your hands full with her!" She's a crazy mortal!"
 He looks at the others, telling them to back off.

Donna Tischner

Just as the Pilot says, "We are descending, please buckle up."

Everyone sits and buckles up, and Roman comes back into the room, telling me to put my seat belt on.

As the plane lands into the darkness down the runway, we get off stepping into a waiting limousine. Roman has me by my arm, guiding me onto the seat. He holds my forearm the whole drive. Almost 2 hours and we approach the castle. Sitting high on the mountains, surrounded by water and trees. Guards stand at the perimeter. It's like a Fortress.

As we drive up the mountain, the car finally comes to a stop. Servants stand outside in the cold to greet Roman and his entourage.

I look at this castle in reverence; it's like a fairytale. As we step into the foyer, a staircase that is so overwhelmingly powerful, you walk up 8 steps, it veers to the left and the right. The Dark Blue carpet lines the center of the stairs with gold trim. Rod iron black banister that swirls flowingly up the white marble columns. It's the most beautiful design I have ever seen. Breathtaking.

Kiss Of Life

Roman leads me up the many stairs to my room. "You're on the third floor." He said to me.

He unlocks the door, and we enter.
I look at my room in solemn, it's beautiful and enormous. My bed sits on a platform, with a built-in cornice around the bed's perimeter and Dark blue Royal Drapes hanging. Columns stand on the platform, near the bed lined in gold trim.

Matching French sofas and antique tables, trimmed also in gold.

Then he says, "I'm on the fourth floor." He takes my hand, bringing me to his room. He unlocks his door, going in, another room of epoch!

His room is Wrapped in Red velvet drapes. His bed is a canopy laced in gold. The setting is that of a King.

Roman tells me, "I will send for you shortly, but you must go to your room now." I look at him, feeling aggrieved. Then walk down to my room.
I enter my room, throwing my purse on my bed. Sitting there thinking, now what am I supposed to do?

I decided to check out the rest of my quarters. The bathroom is all marble. A tub that sits on a platform and dark drapes that block out the sunlight.

I look in my closet. Gowns in every style and color. Long and short ones. Jewelry I thought only queens could have. I pick up the diamond necklace, holding it between my fingers, then throw it down. I don't even care about this. I walk out of the closet and sit on the French sofa. It's all stunning, but lonely.

Then there's a knock at my door. I open it up, seeing Belvidere. He brings in my luggage, asking if he could get me anything; I tell him, my own personal bar with all the liquor we have in the Castle. He asks me if I really want that; when I tell him yes, he leaves the room.

A few minutes later, Roman comes in asking me why I need a bar; I tell him so I can get drunk! Then he says to me, "I'm going to give you a tour of the castle; there are some places you are forbidden to enter." He wraps his arm around mine and leads us downstairs. He shows me the kitchen and the Drawing Room. Showing me another parlor and pool room. The castle is so large I can see myself getting lost in it. He takes me to the dining room, telling me to be dressed for dinner this evening. Letting

Kiss Of Life

go of my arm, he tells me to get ready. I give him a look. Back in my room, I pull out a Long black off-the-shoulder gown. Do my hair and makeup and open my bedroom door.

When I step out, Roman greets me, entwining his arm in mine, escorting me downstairs to the dining room. We enter, and Roman walks me to my seat, pushing in my chair; Roman sits next to me at the head, and then everyone else sits.

The room is full. 20 Vampires sit at the long table. Candelabras border the length with fine china and Crystal bottles filled with plasma. Thorny Black and Red Roses sit in vases bordering the spread. It's eerie but elegant.

Servers bring in our meals and pour our drinks. Everyone waits for me to taste the food first; once I approve, they begin to eat.

I find myself playing with my food. As one vampire stares at me. I look down the length of the table, noticing him; I'm thinking, it's, Skid. He gets up, walking over to me, and I look up at him, Roman asks,

"What is it?"
 "I came down here to introduce myself, to your lady

friend."
Skid looks at me, I put my hand out to shake his, but he kisses the top of my hand, saying,
"I'm Skid. It's a pleasure to meet you."

Smiling, I say, "The pleasure is all mine." Skid then says, "You are Ravishing." I squint my eyes, and Roman says, "That's enough, Skid, take your seat."
But instead, he leaves the room.

Then Roman questions why I'm not eating, saying, "You do not approve of the meal?" I tell him, "It's fine; I just have other things on my mind."

I ask him if I can be excused, and he gets annoyed. Have a drink with us, he tells me. When I agree, we go into the Parlor.

Roman hands me my drink. I stand near a window, looking out and sipping my wine. When Skid approaches me, saying, "How did you end up with Romania?" Smiling, I tell him, "Roman has ways."

Skid laughs, spilling his drink of plasma on me. I jump back. Thick red blood drips down my neck. My arms and my gown. *I look like Carrie from the movie.*

Kiss Of Life

Skid gets a look in his eye. I begin to feel nervous and attempt to leave the room to shower. Roman notices and asks, "How did this happen?" I tell Roman, "It was an accident." Roman watches me exit the room. Behind me, Skid. He's following me.

I manage to get halfway up the stairs, and Skid corners me. He traps me with his arms boxing me in, saying, "You should be with a man, someone who knows how to treat you; I'd never lock you in a room." "I am with a man." "No. that's not a man. A man would be licking the blood off you like this." Skid takes my arm, holding it, and licks the blood off my arm, I tried to pull it away from him, but I couldn't.

I ask Skid, "Let me go before Roman catches you." Just then, Roman pulls him off me. He yells at me to go to my room. I'm so irritated; I run up the rest of the stairs to my room, locking the door.

Roman grabs Skid by the throat, yelling at him to stay away from me, then he throws him down the stairs, sliding across the floor. Skid is angry. Roman sees and says to him, "Is there something you want to say to me?" But Skid stands to his feet, fixing his clothes and walks away.

Not long after, Roman is knocking at my door, telling me to open it. I open the door, and he walks in. I only have a towel on, Roman's eyes glance over my body and back to my face. He says, "I thought you didn't like Skid? what was that I just witnessed? were you enjoying him?"

I'm in shock by his question. I can't even speak. Shaking my head back and forth at him, I say, "I cannot believe you would even ask me such a thing! he trapped me on the stairs." "Trapped you? he was licking you!"

I close my eyes, take a deep breath. I feel the hairs standing up on the back of my neck; I walk away from him. Roman yells, "Don't walk away from me!" I stop. Look at him. Then bow and curtsey, saying, "Yes, master!"

Now I really pissed him off! He grabs me, throwing me on my bed and ripping off my towel. I try to cover my naked body with my hands. Yelling at him to stop. But he grabs me, holding my head, then bites my neck. It's mean. It's brutal. It's scary.

Now my blood is pouring down my shoulder, dripping on the bed, and I see it all over Roman's face.

I start thinking, I despise you! I resent you so much! Why

Kiss Of Life

am I here? He's reading my mind. I'm trying not to let him into my thoughts, but he manages to hear them. "Why did you bring me here? Why do you want me with you?" I turn over, grabbing the blankets to cover myself, and he leaves the room. Sobbing hysterically, I stay on the bed, falling asleep.

In the morning, I don't go to breakfast. Roman asks Belvidere, "Where is Jewels?" He replies, "She hasn't come down yet." Then the Castle shakes and vibrates with strength and force that everyone in the house feels, they begin to worry about us.

I get out of bed, shower, and get dressed. But I still refuse to go down. I've been so wrapped up in everything I hadn't noticed that Belvidere brought me in my own personal bar. Stocked with wines and other fine liquors. Smiling to myself, I thank him quietly.

Seconds later, my door is being broken down. Roman is standing in the vestibule. He crosses the threshold, grabbing me. Pulling me to the hall, but I fight him telling him I won't go! Again, the house starts shaking; he yells, "You're so defiant of me! Why?" "You treat me horribly!" "Let's go now! you're coming to breakfast!"

Roman shoves me to the broken door, pushing me to the

steps. We enter the dining room, and I sit for breakfast. All the others are waiting to be seated to eat. Then Roman makes me apologize to them. I stand, keeping my eyes down but my head up. I say,

"My apologies for keeping you all waiting; it won't happen again."

Then I look at Roman and ask him,
"Are you satisfied now?"
Roman slams his fist on the table, causing the food and dishes to vibrate. I begin to laugh, and then he makes the Castle shake like an Earthquake.

Laughing more, I then sit. But Roman grabs me by the back of my hair, gripping it so tight, he pulls me out of the room like that into the Parlor, and asks me why I am mocking him, but I can't help but laugh more. He slaps me so hard across the face, I fall to the floor with a bloody mouth.

Laying on the floor wiping my blood off my mouth, I look up at him, saying,
"You're an asshole. Why don't you just finish me now because I can't stand you anymore!"

Kiss Of Life

Roman stares down at me, then says, "I plan on it." And walks away.

Sometime later, Roman leaves on business, and I sit in the drawing-room alone. Tess approaches me, asking, "What happen to your neck?" I shrug my shoulder. But she already knows what happen by the marks. I ask her not to bring it up again. We sit and talk for a while. When others come in.

A gorgeous older vampire walks over to me, saying, "I'm Raven, you are one tough mortal! I have never seen any mortal talk to Romanian the way you have." "I apologize, but we shouldn't discuss him; he wouldn't want us to." She laughs amusingly, saying, "Nonsense, I can talk about anyone I want." She flings her hair over her shoulder, then saying; "even his wife talked about him." I stand, trying to excuse myself, but they ask me to stay. Raven talks more about Roman's deceased wife.

"She was stunning! Her hair, long dark, like yours. Her eyes, bluer than blue. Her body was unbreakable, perfect in every way. And her personality? Serious, stern, and demanding!" "Demanding?" I asked. "Yes, whatever she wanted, she got, and if she didn't approve of something, everyone in the house knew it meant trouble."

"I don't think we should talk about her! Roman will be mad!"

"You should know about her, Justina, was like you! A hand full! Trouble."

"I beg your pardon." I'm not trouble! I just want to be treated fairly! I want to be respected! I must go. Excuse me."

I exit the room leaving the others gasping.

Making my way to my bedroom, showering, and preparing for dinner tonight.

Tess and Raven continue to talk about me. Raven speaks, saying, "She wants to be treated fairly? What the hell does she expect? Romanian will never let a mortal rule him." Tess replies, "I would be very meticulous how you talk about her; this one is special to him; I have seen it." Raven waves her hand at Tess, telling her, "Nonsense, it's just a madder of time before he makes her like us." Tess disagrees and excuses herself.

Now nearing the dinner hour, I decide to go to the dining room on my own; I don't need an escort this evening. I

Kiss Of Life

walk down the many stairs into the dining room, and everyone stands. I'm surprised by this but still walk to my seat, standing and waiting for Roman.

When he enters the room, he sees me asking to speak with me for a minute. Huffing and puffing, I walk over to Roman, and he takes me far away from the dining room, saying,

"You deliberately came into the dining room without me; why?"

"Nothing I do is good enough for you; if I don't come to dinner, you rip me apart; if I go without you, you rip me apart! Why do you care if I didn't wait for you? I'm here, aren't' I?"

"It is disrespectful to my guest and me; we will always walk into the dining room together!" "I had enough of you; I want to go home! I don't think I can take any more of this!" "You will remain here!"

Roman grabs me pushing my back up against the wall, scolding me about wanting to go home. And telling me I should be more respectful of him and his house.

He takes my arm entwined in his, and we enter the dining

room together. He pushes in my chair, I sit, then everyone else does too.

After dinner, another Vampire approaches me, He tells me his name introducing himself as John Taylor. John takes my hand kissing it, then bringing me to a chair to sit.

He talks about Romanian, saying, they have been friends for over 150 years, and how they met in Transylvania in a saloon.

He says,
"back in those days, life was simpler. No internet, phones, or Television. If you wanted to know something, you read the papers. But today, things have been made known to anyone who wants to find something out."

I say to John,
"Why are you telling me this?"

He responds saying, "everything I wanted to know about you, I looked up."

"I'm sorry?"

"I have learned, your father was a detective, and has

passed away not too long ago. And your mother? A music teacher. She too has passed. You, you worked in Manhattan NY as a teacher as well."

"I'm sorry, why are you telling me this?"
"You should know that every Vampire will know who you are and will want to know the woman in Romanian's life."

"I don't care about any of that, I don't care who knows about me, and I don't care what's being said about me. I only know, I need to get out of here! Now, if you'll excuse me, we're done speaking of this."

"You might want to change your tone little girl. You can be eaten alive at any second!"

"Are you threatening me? I didn't ask you about your life, why do you care about mine?"

"I want to be sure you are right for my mentor Romanian, and you're not going to hurt him!"

"Me? Hurt him, are you kidding?"
I put my hand to his face telling him to stop talking. I leave the room abruptly running up the stairs to my room and slamming the door.

Donna Tischner

When Roman hears the commotion, seeking out answers he enters my bedroom. Looking at me with the stare of death. Asking questions. Then stalking me. He comes at me with destruction in his eyes and I fall back onto the bed.

"Why can't you just behave like a normal girl? Why can't you stay out of trouble for one day! Why am I always in her scolding you?" He yells and yells and doesn't stop.

The others listen attentively, as I whimper on my bed. Finally, I say to him,
"That's what you would hear, what you would think. You only see what you want to see!

Why did you make me come here? Why can't you let me be? Just get out!" I protested.

 I stand to my feet and begin punching him so violently he grabs my wrist, with one swift move, squeezing them leaving bracelet marks on me. Roman's stops breathing for a few seconds, and then his fangs descend, his eyes turn red, and his skin turns a grey with thick veins popping out. I have never seen this before.

Kiss Of Life

Roman is on top of me, saliva pools from his mouth, and blood shines in his eyes.
I feel his nails digging into my flesh, like knives. I scream, moving my face away from him, trying to shift my body away from his.

I scream again, crying, "Oh God!"

Belvidere comes running into my room attempting to pull Roman off me. Roman throws him back. Belvidere hits the floor. Again, Belvidere grabs Roman saying, "It's okay, come." He tries to calm him down.

I jump off the bed taking cover in a corner.

Belvidere leads Roman to his room talking with him explaining, she has done nothing wrong, everyone keeps coming at her, and she politely excuses herself. You need to listen to her more.

Roman is so irate, he lashes out at Belvidere telling him to get out!

2 days pass, and neither of us have left our rooms.

I cried so much my eyes have swelled up and my nose is torn. I've been drinking and now all I want to do is sleep.

Donna Tischner

Roman has had time to think about everything transpiring. And now has calmed down enough to emerge from his room.

I wake the next morning to Tessa knocking at my door. I tell her to come in and she sits on the edge of my bed asking how I am. I tell her I'm fine asking of she's seen Roman. She tells me, he hasn't been downstairs in 2 days now. I lay on the bed and feel the tears rolling off my cheeks, when Tessa says, "Why don't you take a shower and clean yourself up, join us in the parlor for afternoon drinks." I tell her, "I don't want to see Roman, I'm not ready yet." But she replies, "Maybe it's better to see him and make peace, so everyone can be together." After a minute of thinking about what Tessa said, I respond to her,
"Okay, I'll be down soon then."

Feeling embarrassed by my outburst the other day, I continue to dress. Wondering if Roman will be joining us this morning, I make my way down to the parlor. Staring off into the distance.
I notice everyone looking my way, whispering, and then laughing. I feel, they dislike me and want me out of the Castle, and out of Romanian's life, but I remain there, by

Kiss Of Life

Roman's demands. Not like I have a choice.

Donna Tischner

Chapter 8:
TRUCE

Sitting in the drawing-room sipping my drink, I decide to get up and look at the pictures on the wall when I see this portrait of Roman and his parents. A painting by an unknown artist back in the 14th century. The painting is stunning. The lighting is low, and his parents are sitting on throne chairs.

Roman walks over to me; I sneak a look at him, turning my head quickly away. As upset with him as I am, I'm still very attracted to him. Actually, still in love with him...

He puts his hand on the small of my back, explaining the painting to me. I smile politely at him. Then say,

"It's beautiful." Then he asks,
"how have you been?"
"Fine."

I stare into his eyes, I know he's reading my thoughts, so

Kiss Of Life

I move a little, making space between us.

Trying to throw him off. But he realizes what I am doing and says,

"I can still read you, no madder how far away you move." I can only respond,
"I know..."

Then I try to excuse myself, saying,

"excuse me for a moment."

But he pulls my arm, tugging me closer to him. He reaches down and kisses me. I kiss him back, but there's no passion or feelings behind the kiss. He senses it. Then he says,

"We need a truce."
"A truce?"
"Yes..."
"What are you proposing?"
"A quiet evening on my terrace tonight."
"Why, why do you want to be with me?"

Roman shakes his head, saying,

"I'm trying to make peace; can't you just acknowledge

that?"

"I do acknowledge that, but after everything, I don't know anymore."

"You're impossible, have dinner with me?"

Standing before Romanian, I breathe heavy, sighing, I look down at the floor, then tell him,

"I don't trust you; you're going to hurt me or something, bite me, slap me, or throw me into a wall. Why would I put myself in that position again, being alone with you, frightens me now!"
"You forced me to do those things, and that isn't my intention for this evening."
"I forced you? You're unbelievable! Fine, I'll be there. Pardon me."

Roman watches me leave the room. Going up the stairs.

I have been holding my breath that entire time; when I get in my room, I let it out! Breathing again. My heart is pounding so fast; I thought I was going to collapse.

I shower and look for something to wear; opening the

closet, I don't even want to have dinner with him, but I have no choice, I choose something black. A long Chiffon gown that's form fitting, with sheer flowing lace that drags along the floor. Long sleeves that fall off the shoulders. Black stilettos and a black onyx necklace. I grab a bottle of wine from my bar and walk up to the fourth floor to Roman's room knocking.

He opens the door. He's wearing a black Gothic Victorian Frock Coat, Gentlemen Punk Simple Trousers, and a Gothic Lace Flocking Shirt. His muscles protrude out of his coat, and he smells delicious. I enter his room, giving him a peck on his cheek. He takes me by my hand, leading us out to the terrace. He had arranged candles and chocolates set up with fresh flowers and strands of lighting around the columns.

He pulls out a chair for me to sit, then pours us some wine. He sits, placing his hand on my knee. I can already feel my body reacting to him. I realize he's trying to make this work.
He looks at me and says, "Truce?" My eyes get soft. And a smile forms on my lips. I feel a little relaxed, and reply, "Truce..." Then he asks, "How can we make this work?"

"You don't want to hear my answer; it will only upset you."

Donna Tischner

"Talk to me," he spoke.
I begin to say how I feel.
"You are everything to me, and I know I could love you so much more. But I can't be treated like an animal.

You are locking me up in my room all the time. The way you bite me, you're going to kill me. Strangling me, this can never work if you continue to hurt me. I feel deceived, neglected of your love, and defeated."
He stares at me, then a smile forms on his lips; he stands holding the baluster railing looking off into the distance, then he turns to me and says, "We don't even know each other that much, why don't you tell me something about yourself."

I put my wine down on the table and ask him, "What would you like to know?" "Anything, what type of music do you like?" I squint my eyebrows together, thinking, *this is weird but okay*. Then I tell him, "Jazz mostly, but I enjoy all types, classical, pop and rock." What were you like as a child?"

I begin to realize where this is going and just go with it telling him, "I was an only child, I never asked for much, I didn't cry when I got hurt, I never caused a scene when I

Kiss Of Life

didn't get my way, and I always accepted what I had. My parents were exceptionally good to me."

Roman thinks about what I just told him, then says, "You never asked your parents for anything?" "Sure, I did, but nothing unimaginable; I asked for a car when I started driving; I asked for a stereo when I was a teenager."

"Did you get the car?" "Yes, not the one I wanted, but I got a car. I worked and bought my own things once I was old enough to."

Continuing, I tell him, "Roman, I know what you're doing; I wasn't a spoiled brat. I didn't care about miscellaneous things. I'm not a spoiled brat now; I only want your respect, that's all."

Roman gets quiet. Then tells me, "I fear for your safety, that's why I locked you up. I don't want the others to try anything, to hurt you. I didn't know how to act when you didn't show up for breakfast the other morning. I was humiliated in front of our guests.

I apologize to you. I know I was wrong. I promise not to hurt you again. Will you still be with me? I don't want to lose you.

I felt dreadful after you saw me as a demon. Can you

Donna Tischner

forgive me?

Give me another chance to make it up to you? I never felt this way for any woman, especially a mortal woman. It has been decades since I was with anyone, being with you, this is different for me, you're the only one who has ever spoken back to me."
Roman stands there, watching my expressions, waiting for me to reply, then he turns towards the railing. The wind pushes his hair back, and his scent is blown in my direction, making me vulnerable.

I think my heart did a flip when Roman said this to me; I think he touched my soul, and I saw the universe in a whole new light.

I stand to my feet, placing my hands on Roman's forearms; I look him in his eyes, telling him, "All I want is for you and me to be together; I am so enamored with you!"

He bent down, holding my back, and kisses me. This time I kissed him with passion and felt the emotion in his kiss too. I felt the love I know he has for me.
My feelings for him have been saved by his apology.

Kiss Of Life

He holds me tightly, clutching me, saying how sorry he is for how he has treated me. I tell him, "Never speak of this again; it's a new day."

He takes my hand, leading us into his room, kissing me than laying me down on his bed. In his excitement, he begins to undress me.

Sliding his hands down my back, grabbing a fist full of my hair, and sucking on my neck.

I unbutton his slacks, pulling them down, one hip at a time. He moans in his pleasure, kissing my breasts and dragging his tongue over my throat.
He asks me, "Can I taste your blood?" "Looking into his hypnotizing eyes, I reply, "Yes."

Licking my neck and massaging my bottom, he pierces me softly; I feel no discomfort. He leaves the area clean and swiftly gets on top. His hips move slowly on me, and I squeeze his ass enduring him snug to my body.

My nails dig into his back, and Roman embraces my lips; he traces his mouth to my cheek then whispers in my ear, "You're so beautiful."

I kiss his neck and his chest as my hands slip into his hair, my legs open wider for him, he leaves me panting, I grab the back of his head and he slips in between my breasts covering them in kisses, my cries of pleasure cut through the silence. Roman concludes. It's both luscious and compassionate.
He lies on top of me for some time, holding me, and then he tells me.

"You mean everything to me. I hold an incredibly special place for you in my heart. I never want to fight like that again."
I push Roman back a little to see his eyes and then tell him,
"Roman, I love you." He keeps me close to him throughout the night.

In the morning, we dress for breakfast. We walk into the dining room together, and everyone is stunned, staring at us, and whispering amongst themselves. Roman tells them to calm down in a laughing manner.
As breakfast is served and we eat, Roman makes an announcement,
"I have decided to grant Amnesty to Skid." There's talking and whispering at the table.

Kiss Of Life

"He's been locked up for a few days now, and he has assured me, there will be no more trouble from him." I look at Roman, wink my eye at him, and continue to eat. He rubs my hand. Smiling at me, asking me if I'm alright. I tell him I'm fine sipping my juice.

When breakfast is finished, I remain in my chair, and Roman waits for me to stand. But I stay sitting. He puts his hand on my shoulder, asking if I'm coming, but I tell him soon. For some reason, I just can't get up; I'm glued in my seat thinking about Skid's amnesty.
Tessa comes into the dining room asking me if I'm upset over Skid being set free; I just tell her, "I'm fine, it'll be fine..." I stand pushing out my chair and taking Tessa's arm in mine, going into the drawing-room.

Soon after our arrival, Skid comes walking in. He sees me, then smiles big. I feel my stomach turn. I leave going to my bedroom. Roman notices me leaving and stops me. Asking, "Where are you going?"

"To my room for a minute." "Why?" "Roman, you're doing it again. I'll be back."

But when I get upstairs, I don't go back down. I sit on my couch, grabbing a pillow pulling on the tassels, and placing it on my lap. I stay there for the remainder of the

afternoon.
As I loll on the sofa, I begin to feel like I'm not alone in my room. I feel like there are eyes on me. As I stay seated, I look around the room. Still feeling uneasy, I get up. I open my closet, look in the bathroom, under my bed, behind the curtains, and even under the furniture. But no one is in the room. I start to think it's just me being paranoid. I sit back down. Then I notice a small hole in the wall. I get up close to it, put my eye to it, and another eye is staring back at me. I jump back and fall, landing on my ass. My heart is racing. Within minutes, Roman is walking into my room. He sees me on the floor. Grabbing my hand, he lifts me, asking what happen.

I tell him about the hole, and he walks over to the wall, putting his eye to the spot, then rubs his finger over it. He tells me he'll check it out from the other room. Roman leaves going to the room. But the room is empty. No furnishings, nothing.

He tells me to sleep in his room until the hole is patched up.
Feeling creeped out that someone has been watching me, Roman tells me not to go back into my room until he gets to the bottom of this.

Kiss Of Life

After dinner, everyone gathers in the drawing-room for drinks. Tessa and I talk, and Roman observes everyone. He has his suspicions about who it can be. He watches as some leave the room and comes back. He notices who is looking at me. And he eyes who is speaking with me.

By bedtime, as I drift off, Roman gets out of bed and goes into the empty room waiting. But no one reenters the room. He climbs into bed with me and holds me tight.

When I wake, I go to my room for a change of clean clothes. Roman is still asleep. I walk in and go to my closet, taking out a pretty blue dress and low heels for breakfast. Only when I turn to put the shoes down is someone behind me.

I fall, letting out a scream. A man is standing in my bedroom. I get up, ask him, "can I help you?" he stares at me, then says,
"I am Semie, a business partner of Romans."

"Okay, why are you in my room?"
 "We need to talk."
"Talk? About what? Roman wouldn't like it if he found you in here."
"Meet me in the Pool room after breakfast."

He turns on his heels and leaves my room. I'm left standing there thinking, there's no way I'm meeting with this guy alone.

Semie is tall, built, and has long brown hair and eyes; he has a hard facial structure, good jawbone, and thick eyebrows. He's wearing a gold crucifix, leather pants, and nothing under his suit jacket, just bare skin. It's kind of sexy.
I grab my clothes and run up the stairs to Roman's room and shower.

After my shower, I sit on the bed drying my hair with my towel, and Roman opens his eyes; he puts his hand on my waist, rubbing it up and down, then says, "You're trembling, why?" I turn to him and say, "No, I'm not." He sits up, looks me in my eyes, and says, "Tell me! what is it?" I get off the bed, telling him, "everything is fine," and go back into the bathroom.

 After we dress, Roman takes my hand in his and says to me, "I know something is going on with you, you're doing a good job blocking your thoughts from me, tell me at once, what is it?" I respond by saying, "everything is okay. don't worry." I kiss Roman on his cheek and take his hand, leading us into the dining room.

Kiss Of Life

Once finished with breakfast, everyone goes about their day. Roman leaves to attend his business, and I go into the drawing-room. While I'm sitting in there, Semie comes over to me asking, "why I didn't meet him in the pool room," I tell him, there's no way I'm meeting with you alone, I don't even know you." He gets a look in his eye of anger, and I sink into my chair. He sits next to me, clamps his hands together, leaning on his knees, and says, "I have information for you about your precious Romanian you would be inclined to hear." I stand telling him,
"I'm not interested in what you have to say about him, I love him, and I won't let you talk down about him."

"Brave girl you are... You might want to hear this!"
"Thank you, but I'm not interested."

I stand; leaving the room, I walk right into Skid. We collide. I look up at him, apologizing, saying, "excuse me, I'm sorry." But Skid grabs my arms, saying, "You should be more careful where you're walking. What's the hurry, have a drink with me?" "no no, thank you, I need to go." He watches as I run up the stairs.

I go to Roman's room and sit. Thinking about everyone and everything. I need to talk to Roman, where can he

be?
I decide to go look for him. Heading back downstairs, I walk through the long halls. Looking for his office. I turn and end up in the chapel. I stand on the threshold, then take a seat on the pew. Then Semie sits next to me. I lose my breath. Looking at him, I ask, "Why can't you just leave me alone?" I slide away from him. But he glides down the pew. I get mad and ask him,

"Okay, tell me, what is it?"
"Your precious Roman has plans for you."
"I don't think I want to hear this; I should go."
"YOU WILL SIT!"

he said in a stern voice as it echoes through the chapel.

I sit with my heart beating in my hands. Shaking, I begin to send messages to Roman. Come quickly! I'm in trouble.

Semie gets closer to me. I arch my back away from him. Then he says,
"Your Roman will soon be taking your life."
Just then, Roman is standing in front of Semie, with his arms folded and a look in his eye of death." I spring off the pews into the aisle. Roman grabs Semie and has him

Kiss Of Life

brought to the dungeon. Then he asks me,

"What the hell is going on? Why were you in the Chapel?"

"First of all, I was looking for you, I needed to tell you what was happening; second, I stumbled in here looking for your office when Semie followed me."

Roman takes me by my arm, hauling me into his office making me sit.

I learned Roman's office was not far from the Chapel. Then he speaks, saying, "Now tell me, what's going on?"
"Are you going to take my life?"

"Do you want me to?" I feel my eyes go wide, and my mouth moves to the side; I say to him, "No..."
"Then you have nothing to worry about."

Roman then asks me,
"What is going on with you and Semie?"

"He snuck into my room this morning, telling me to meet him in the Pool room after breakfast, but I didn't go. I was looking for you to tell you when I stumbled into the Chapel. That's when Semie found me in there."

Donna Tischner

"Why didn't you tell me this morning? When I asked you, what was wrong?"
"I didn't want to cause any trouble; I'm sorry."
"What did he tell you?" "You are going to take my life."

Roman tells me to get up, and then he walks me back to his room. Asking me to stay here till he returns.

Then he goes to the dungeon to speak with Semie. He is bound by chains that are in the wall. His hands raised above his head, and his feet chained to the floor.

Once there, he asks him, "Why would you tell Jewel I was going to take her life?"

"I never told her that! she's lying!" "Well, Semie, do you want to change your story?" "She doesn't like Vampires, she told me." "You do realize, she likes me. I'm a Vampire." Semie doesn't respond. Roman is aggrieved. He calls in re-enforcements. "I have called on my men to take your life! You will tell me now, what you wanted to tell her!"

Semie puts his head down knowing he cannot win, then tells Roman, "Jeremy, told me about her blood, I wanted to taste it. I lied to her to get her alone."

Kiss Of Life

"Where is Jeremy? Is he here in Romania?"
"Yes."
"Tell me at once, where is he?"

"He's here in the castle, hiding. He's been watching both of you. Spying and listening. He put the hole in Jewel's wall so he would know when she was alone."
Roman leaves the room and his men take Semie's head. Then they surround the Castle. Looking to trap Jeremy.

Jeremy goes from room to room hiding. But he can't keep his charade up for too much longer. When Jeremy steps out into the corridor causing himself to surrender.

Jeremy is brought into the dungeon and questioned about the situation. Roman makes the decision to have him locked up.

Soon Roman tends to other business in the Castle, then leaves to be with me. My door has been fixed and the hole patched up. Roman tells me, it's safe to go back into my room.

Donna Tischner

He kisses me sweetly as we say goodnight going to our separate rooms.

Kiss Of Life

Chapter 9:
BECKETT

As I lay in my bed, I can hear the winds blowing outside. With the darkness and the lightning striking, I begin to wince. I know if there's thunder, there's sure to be lightening.

The winds pick up, and I see the shadow of the trees reflecting in my window. Then the thunder starts, making loud banging sounds.

The powerlines go down, causing the electric to go out.

I grab my covers, hiding my face in them, then I peek out. My heart starts thumping so fast. I'm terrified. I get up and grab my bathrobe from the foot of my bed, then light the candle on my nightstand. The sky is fierce tonight.

Every time the thunderclaps, I jump. I open my bedroom door, then peek out, calling *hello*. I run up the stairs to Roman's room, knock then run in. Roman is standing at the door. I run into his arms, holding him, and he tells me

Donna Tischner

I'm trembling.

Then he tells me to shush, saying, "I'm here." I look up at him in the eerie darkness and tell him how frightened I am. A half-smile beams at his lips, and he leads me to his bed.

He covers me with the blankets, and I yell, "don't leave me!" sitting up in the bed. He walks back over to me and rubs my cheek, saying, "Nothing can happen to you; I'm right here!"

Roman holds a drink in his hand then sits on the sofa. The candles danced in the darkness, and the thunder sings to him.

I watch him from the bed as he enjoys the storm over his head. He blows the candle out and then lays down next to me. Pulling me closer to him. I begin to feel so safe in his arms. Falling asleep.

In the morning, we sit for breakfast while the others talk about last night's storm. Roman and I smile at each other. He knows I was scared to death.

Then Roman tells me he must go away for a few days. I

Kiss Of Life

feel alone already just hearing this.

I ask him, "how long will you be gone?" "3 days at the most." "Can't I come with you?" "I'm afraid not Princess. Tessa and Belvidere will look after you."

I smile and sit in the drawing-room with some of the others. When Roman comes to me saying, "Don't be upset with me, I don't want to leave you being this sad." I stand, taking Roman by his hand, leading him out of the room, then saying to him with a pitiful voice, holding his arms, "I can't lie to you, yes, I am upset, I don't want to be alone with the others, and I am going to miss you terribly."

Roman takes my hand, leading us up the stairs to his room. He kisses me sweetly and affectionately. His lips seek out my jaw, kissing me there. Then my neck. I moan in delight. Making him eager to take me.

I feel his long nails, sending chills through me. I begin to undress him, taking his jacket off. I feel fervent. I stand with my back to his chest. He pulls the sleeve of my dress down, kissing the top of my shoulder.

Roman places his hand around my back and brings me gently down on the bed. Lifting my legs over his shoulder and kissing my inner thighs.

Donna Tischner

I tell him, "Come up here." Roman moves swiftly on top of me. He kisses my neck, my breast, and then I feel the pinch.

His movement is like a slow dance. I grab the sheets wrapping them around my wrists as he squeezes me in his pleasure. He takes delight in seeing me savoring him; he takes delight in hearing me. I think to myself; *I don't want this to end.*

But it's like I said it out loud. He hears my thoughts and continues to please me in every way possible.

I told Roman, "I love you." Wondering, can he ever love me the way I love him. Does he realize my affection for him is real?

Laying on the bed, he holds me. I feel the tears building, and I turn over on my stomach. Roman tells me, "Don't be upset." He strokes the back of my hair, trying to turn me over to look at him. When he does, he sees the tears rolling down my cheeks, asking, "What is it? why the tears?" I put my hand to my face, covering it. He tries to pull my hands off. but all I can do is bury my face in his chest. He holds me telling me to, "Shh."

Kiss Of Life

Not long after, he's leaving for his business trip. Still, he's thinking about me crying. I overhear a conversation between him and Belvidere; he told him, "I'm bothered by her tears, and I don't wish to leave her like this."

Belvidere replies, "Sir, your feelings have grown abundantly for her; I fear she has won your heart."

Roman responds by saying, "Is this love? it has been decades since I've known it."
"I do believe you care for her more than you realize."
"Belvidere, you may be right; what do I do about this now? I wasn't expecting to feel this way for her."

"Sir, that is for you to decide; But I think, you should tell her your true feelings soon."

"Perhaps you are right." Belvidere continues to say, she has all the potential to be your special lady and wife." Roman asks him, "whatever do you mean potential?" "She is beautiful, smart, talented, and stubborn all at the same time." The two of them laugh, then Roman leaves closing the door behind him.

During the night, I make my way to my own bedroom. Getting into bed. Thinking about Roman. I miss him, I tell myself. Falling asleep to the sound of his voice.

By morning I make my way to breakfast. As I enter and take my seat, the others sit after me. Everyone begins to talk. Some asking me when Roman will be back, and some question how I slept without him. Others stare at me, making me feel uncomfortable. I eat, keeping my head down, making no eye contact with them.

Then one of the men comes to sit next to me, saying, "you know, you're lovely." I look up at him and smile, saying thank you." Then he tells me his name saying, "my name is Beckett, let's have a drink later."

"Oh no, thank you, I don't think Roman would approve."
"He won't know!

"Roman knows everything, but I thank you for the offer." Beckett speeds out of the room when Tessa comes to me. I ask her to sit, and we talk for a long time. After dinner, we sit in the parlor drinking and talking more. When we lose track of time. She tells me good night and leaves the room asking if I am coming; when I say I'll be up soon, I'm going to the kitchen first.

I find myself staring into the darkness of the kitchen, looking for the light switch. When I hear a crash of pots falling to the ground. I call out, "hello? is someone there?"

Kiss Of Life

Then I hear the echo of footsteps coming towards me; I turn and run out of the kitchen down the corridor and find a door, slipping into it. I keep running down the dark hall till I find another door opening it. It creeks. I close it and keep on running. I have no idea what part of the castle I'm in, but I'm scared to death. It is entirely dark. The Blackness has me paralyzed.
I don't know who is chasing me, since I didn't see a face.

I take off my shoes, so they don't make noise as I run through the halls. Feeling the coldness on my feet. I realize this must be an ancient part of the castle; no one uses it anymore. I feel the floor coming to a steep hill like I'm going down. And the walls a cold slab of concrete.

I'm shaking as I find another door, quietly opening it and slipping in. I begin to smell an aroma that makes me gag.

I move into the room more, tripping over something. I put my hands out to feel, and I feel the softness of something, and then I feel the puddles. Rubbing my hand on my dress to clean whatever that was.

I crouch down, hiding in the puddle, when I hear him calling me.

His voice sings...

Donna Tischner

"Jewel's. Oh, where oh where can she be?" I stay silent, keeping my head covered. Then the door slams shut. Still, I'm unsure if he is here with me, so I stay quiet.

After about an hour, I breathed, letting out all the air I was holding in.

I start to meditate, calling on Roman, but I know he's on business, and I don't want to keep troubling him. I'm not even sure he'd hear me at this point.

I guess about another hour passes, and I stand to my feet. Feeling my way around the room. I trip once more, landing on a pile of softness again. I put my hand out feeling it when I realize it's dead bodies. I almost screamed. I think the aroma masked my scent from whoever is chasing me, and that's why he didn't know I was there.

I start to feel tired, like I need to sleep, but I can't hide anymore in this room; the smell makes me ill, so I open the door slowly and quietly, feeling my way and finding another door.

I open it and enter into it, scared and shaking, not knowing what to expect once I'm in.

Kiss Of Life

The room feels cold. I can't make it out, but the mildew smell wakes me up some. I walk a little hitting a box with my toes. I stop quickly, hoping he didn't hear the bang. I believe this man wants to hurt me.

I sit on the icy ground and stay there, shivering with coldness. Until I pass out. It's been 2 days I've been down here, wherever "here" is. I wondered if anyone was looking for me. I don't know if it's daytime or nighttime. I've lost track of the hour.

Back in the castle, Roman comes in. As all the servants and guests, stand in a line to welcome him home. He only has one question.

"Where is Jewel's?"
Everyone looks around the room and at each other. Shrugging their shoulders, when Belvidere steps forward, saying, "we have not seen her in 3 days; we have been searching for her."

Roman has the look of madness in his eyes, yelling, "TURN THE CASTLE UPSIDE DOWN! FIND HER! If anyone has touched her, you will pay with your head!"

Roman goes irate, looking in the cellar and the attic.

Going from room to room. When one of the staff members comes to him saying, "Sir, 3 days ago when we entered the kitchen to serve breakfast, many of the pots were on the ground. I fear someone chased her, knocking them down." Roman yells, "Show me!" The servant takes Roman to the kitchen showing him where the pots were on the floor; when Roman traces the steps, he realizes I must have slipped into the dungeon.

He opens the door entering the older part of the castle, looking in all the rooms. Searching for me when he finds my shoe. An entourage of men follows him. Calling my name and desperately searching. When someone yells out, "I've found her!"

Roman speeds to my side; he slides his hands under my limp body and carries me out to his bedroom. He told Belvidere. "She is covered in blood, smells of death, and her body is failing."

Some scream out, "change her; you must make her like us now!" Others tell him to call in a doctor before you make any decisions. Belvidere makes the call to have a doctor look me over first.

They clean me up, buckets of soap and water are brought

Kiss Of Life

into Roman's room. Clean garments and fresh sheets. They make me comfortable.

Soon a doctor is looking me over.
Roman asks the doctor, "Is Jewel going to be alright? will she make it?"

The doctor tells him, "she will need some I'V fluids and maybe antibiotics. She has some gashes on her legs that look infected. I will start the I'V, and we'll take it from there."

Roman begins to question everyone. Asking what brought this all on, why did Jewel end up in the dungeon? and why was that door unlocked?"
Only, no one can tell him anything except for Tessa.

Tessa pulls Roman to a room where they can speak privately. She tells him, "Beckett asked Jewel to have a drink with him, but she declined, and he sped out of the castle angry. I'm not saying for sure he had anything to do with Jewel's disappearing, but that's what I witnessed."
Roman placed his hands on her shoulder, thanking her and saying he'll look into this.

Belvidere sits with Roman in his bedroom. Belvidere speaks to Roman, saying, 4 days have passed now, and she is not showing any signs of improvement."

"Yes, I know Belvidere."

Roman sits at my bedside, holding and rubbing my hand. Talking to me and kissing my forehead. I hang on to his every word. I heard him tell me, "I love you Printesa mea. Wake up for me. I need you."

Finally, after 5 and a half days, I show some signs of improvement. When I open my eyes, the first thing I saw was Roman's pretty face; I smile at him, and he smiles back at me. He bends down, holding me and saying, "you gave me quite a scare."

Smiling, I reach for his face to touch him, he brings it closer to me. Holding Roman's cheeks with my palm. He places his hand over mine, stroking it with his thumb, then leans in and places a kiss on my lips.

Within a few days, I'm up and walking around. Roman has waited patiently to ask me what had happened and how I ended up in the dungeon.

I explained what transpired and that the door to the dungeon was open, only I didn't know it was the dungeon.

Kiss Of Life

Then I ask Roman, "Please don't leave me, I can't be separated from you again."

Roman holds my hand to his lips and kisses the tops of my fingers. Saying, "I will never leave your side again."

Then Roman tells me, "tonight, I have a surprise for you." I smile shyly, asking, "what is it?" But Roman stands there smiling back and says, "Dress for dinner, and you will soon see."

By dinner, Roman takes my hand and leads me to a veranda outside overlooking the mountain tops. As the cool air breathes down my back and through my hair. I take in the evening sky, looking up to it with my eyes shut and my face exposed to the stars. Smiling appreciatively.

Roman is pleased in his doings and asks me if I'd like some wine; when I say yes, he pours me a glass.

He brings me over to the railing and points out various parts of the countryside, informing me about it. And telling me some of its histories.

Bucovina, a region in Romania, is famous for its monasteries. Roman pointed in the direction.

Donna Tischner

Bihor Massif, Romanian mountain massif, is the highest part of the Apuseni Mountain.

As he points these areas out to me, I begin to realize the history here and learn to appreciate it more with great gratitude.

Soon we are being served dinner, and Roman takes my hand holding it. I tilt my head to him with a smile asking, "is everything alright?" He stares at me for a long time before answering, then stands and walks over to me kneeling in front of me, taking my hands, he says,
"I am so in love with you." As he squeezes my hands in his, he continues to say, "I am so sorry for all I had put you through, you deserve so much better, so much more. I want to be the one to give it to you."

I feel my eyes watering up and then a tear falls landing on Roman's hand. He leans in and kisses me.

I stand and hold him, wrapping my arms around his neck, saying, "Thank you."
After dinner, he takes me on a walk around the grounds, Showing me different property parts. Roman holds my hand tightly as we walk the land; I feel at peace with him.

Kiss Of Life

As Roman and I walk, Roman begins to pick up various scents. As his senses are heightened in his form.

He pulls me close to his body, then says, " Stay close to my side; we are not alone. We need to head back to the Castle."

I latch onto his arm so tight as he walks with me amazingly fast back into the Castle. He has guards take me to his room and wait with me until his return.

Roman has the ability to speed swiftly through the night without being seen or heard; with his newfound blood, he can pick up the smallest insect in a room. Knowing his own abilities, he seeks out the source of his uneasiness. Grabbing the predator with his bare hands and flinging him into the Castle's walls.

When he picks the predator back up by his neck, he realizes it is Beckett. Asking him, "Where have you been? Why are you spying on me?"

Beckett replies, "I thought you were someone else. I didn't know it was you and your lady friend walking the grounds."

Again, Roman asks him, "Where have you been for the past week?"

Donna Tischner

"I went home!"
"Why would you leave and not tell anyone?"

But before Beckett can answer, Roman, picks something else up on him. He can smell my scent.

"You are hiding something; empty your pockets at once!"

Roman ordered.

Beckett begins to take the items from his jacket pocket out, throwing them to the ground. When Roman sees something that catches his eyes, he bends down, picking it up. He holds it in front of his face yelling, "Why do you have this? this belongs to Jewel! This is her scarf."

Then something begins to happen to Roman; he begins to see a vision of that night, the night I was chased into the dungeon. The whole scene plays out as if he were seeing it firsthand.

He grabs Beckett by the throat, telling him he can see how he scared Jewel in the kitchen and how she ran, slipping into a doorway and hiding for dare life. "This was you're doing?"

Without another thought, Roman's increased strength causes him to squeeze Beckett's neck right off his shoulders.

Roman stands there, staring down at his dead body. He begins to think about what he witnessed in that vision; feeling sad, he turns and saunters back into the Castle.

As Roman is walking up the stairs, he sees more visions; he sees how Skid boxed me in on the steps and how Jeremy went to bite me, and how I was speaking the truth. More images play out in his head, and he realizes they're not stopping. He sees his mother and father, his two brothers, and their deaths. Roman collapses on the stairs, holding his head, trying to make it stop. But the visions keep coming.

Donna Tischner

Chapter 10:
THE HAUNTINGS

Roman has more visions as the days go on. Realizing it's my blood, he decides not to endeavor anymore.

The more visions Roman has, the more he learns from everyone. Knowing their secrets and their plans. Roman chooses to keep this information to himself.

His powers have increased, and he cannot control them. When he sees me, I get the impression he wants to rip me apart. I've been keeping my distance. I miss him so much, and I can't even tell him. I want to be with him and hold him, but I can't.

I send Roman messages telepathically. Letting Roman know I'm here for him if he needs me. Only, I never get a response back from him.

A few days have passed, and Roman's visions have

Kiss Of Life

calmed down some. They're not coming in as frequent. Roman seeks me to say how much he has missed me and mentions he had received my messages.

Our reunion is sweet. I kiss Roman all over his face, and he smiles, kissing me back. But the reunion is short-lived, when a wave of visions starts to attack him, I step back, but he sees something and tells me to leave the room. I beg him to let me stay and help him, his face begins to turn into something hideous, and his color a grey I never want to see again.

His nails start to grow so long they're like knives. And his eyes open more extensive, they're blood red. He's changing right before my eyes, and there's nothing I can do.

I leave his room, locking the door so no one can get in. I know, he wouldn't want anyone to see him like that.

The following day the others are questioning me about Roman and his well-being. I tell them he ate something fowl and has been ill. But they start to think I did something to him.
 Tessa asks, "What did he eat?" I tell her I don't know. Raven asks, "Did you do something to our father?" I feel

my eyes widen. I wince in my chair. Telling her, "I assure you; I have done nothing to him! and don't ever ask me that again!" Within a second, Raven speeds to my side, asking me if I'm threatening her.

When Roman enters the room, in a stern voice telling Raven to sit her ass down! And don't ever get in Jewel's face like that again.

Roman stands at the side of my chair and leans down to kiss me. I look up at him, then standing; I hold him asking how he is. He winks at me and sits.

Later as the day turns to evening, Roman and I are walking upstairs to his room when he has another vision. I hold his arm, asking, "Are you having a vision?" Roman sits on the steps and waits for it to pass. Then he looks at me. I ask him again, "Are you alright? " He stands, taking my hand, saying, "Let us continue to my room."

In the Morning, Raven is yelling, "What the hell is going on here?" When Roman and I step out to see what all the commotion is, she approaches me and grabs my wrist, holding me; Roman screams at her to let me go, when she does; she is holding my brooch in her hand, accusing Lincoln and me of sharing a bed while Roman was ill.

Kiss Of Life

One by one, the guest steps out of their rooms to see what is transpiring.

Feeling my eyes widen and my heart thump, I shake my head, back and forth saying, "NO."

I stand there in shock, swearing I have never even spoken to him before. But Raven persists. "You WHORE! we should take your head right now!"

I look at Roman, saying, "You have to believe me! I never!"

Roman Stands firm, telling me to get to my room with a stern and meaningful voice. I run-up to my room, slamming the door.

Then Raven tells Roman she found this on my nightstand, holding Lincoln's Ring out to him. Roman takes the Ring asking Lincoln if this belongs to him. When he says yes, Lincoln swears to Roman he would never disrespect him in such a manner.

Raven stalks Lincoln pointing her index finger at him, calling him a liar!

Lincoln's fangs descend, showing her, he is angry, and he will not stand for another word to leave Raven's mouth. Lincoln grabs Raven throwing her to the floor, banging her head repeatably on the marble tiles. It takes 4 other Vampires to pull him off her and subduing him.

Lincoln stands guarded, telling Roman, "I have never even spoken one word to Jewel. This is all a lie! Jewel has never even looked at me in such a fashion!"

Raven wails, "We have the proof!" When Roman yells out, "ENOUGH!"
Then he tells the guards to release Lincoln and detain Raven.

But she goes ballistic, screaming, "Restrain me? are you mad?"
The guards take Raven to the dungeon and lock her up. As she yells and screams to release her.

Then Roman approaches Lincoln, telling him he knows he is innocent. Then he tells everyone else, "It's over; go back to your rooms."

Soon Roman is approaching me in my room; I run to him, swearing, I'm innocent, but he puts his finger to my lips,

Kiss Of Life

telling me, "shh, I believed you right from the start."
I grab Roman, hugging him. He tells me he saw it all happen. I look at him, asking, "A vision?"
Then he explains to me.

Raven walked into my room going through my jewelry and taking my Blood brooch pin. Then she went into Lincoln's room and puts it on his nightstand. Raven grabs Lincoln's Ring and puts it on my dresser. Leaving the room, she waited.

Roman leaned over to me from the sofa and kissed me, then telling me, I know you wouldn't hurt me like that. My wife, Justina, did. I hold Roman's hand, rubbing my thumb over his, listening.

Justina was very stubborn; she hated that I left on business all the time and told me I was neglecting her and her needs. She sought out different prospects, and they lay in our bed.

I begin to feel my eyes tearing up. And my heart beats faster.
Roman continues.
One night after my return, I found her in bed. She wasn't alone. Another immortal man was with her.

I swallowed, and my tears fell on our hands. Roman hears my heart beating faster and asks, "should I stop?" "No." Roman stands, then begins to pace the floor.

"I didn't know who to grab first, Justina or Rice.
But I grabbed Rice. He showed me no respect, no lament, nothing.

I wanted to drain him, but I wouldn't allow myself to touch his blood. Instead, I ripped his head off his shoulders, and Justina screamed. Seconds after that, I took her life."

Swallowing some more, I was speechless. Motionless. Roman stared into my eyes and said, "I feel what you are feeling; your heart speaks to mine, in a way, none has ever. You are truly sincere and compassionate."

I kissed him on his lips then told Roman, "I am so sorry." Crying on his shoulder, he holds me.

Then Roman told me, "I loved her. She was as you are. Different. Special. But soon, I began to see a change in her. She wanted more. Money. Jewelry, more servants. Her list was never-ending. I gave her everything she wanted. But it still wasn't good enough for her. I felt like I

Kiss Of Life

was drifting away. Her moods became unbearable. I would leave on business on purpose, to escape her. She wouldn't talk to me, and we couldn't work it out. She became greedy, and that tore us apart."

I felt my eyes getting soft. And told Roman, "I will never hurt you; I will never let us get to that point. Still, my heart weighs heavy for your pain, and the wounds you endured."

Roman then told me, "Rice was like a brother to me. When I saw him in bed, my heart shattered? More so because it was him with Justina. I loved him.

When I stared down at his dead body, I almost felt human as the sadness took over. Then I looked down at Justina's body, and I felt emptiness.

I walked out of the room that night and told my Butler to remodel the whole 4th floor.

Gazing in Roman's eyes I begin to see his pain; feeling a sense of grief, I hold him. When he stands, taking my hand and rocks us back and forth, holding me. Then thanking me.

***

Donna Tischner

As Roman makes his way to the dungeon to speak to Raven, I wait in my room for his return.

Raven's rusted chains are barricaded to the brick wall. Her arms over her head. Her legs tiring from standing. As her head hangs down in the cold chamber, she watches as the starved rats await her blood or her death.

As the sconces burn on the slabs of masonry. Candles provide a small pocket of light illumination.

Hooks hang near the chamber doors with corrosion. More chains hang from the ceiling swaying back and forth, making jingling sounds. Enabled to move up and down.

A pool of congealed blood lies near an unusual instrument of torture.

Buckets of dirty water sit on the floor, and bloody rags line the table of torment.
Raven lifts her head, eyeing her soon-to-be agony. Her fate lies in the hands of her father, Romanian Vlad the 3rd. His ruthlessness is wicket, and his compassion, naught.

Kiss Of Life

Romanian never tolerated liars and thieves, but most of all, he despises deceivers of their evil doings.

Roman's footsteps echo down the corridor. Raven hears him coming and braces herself. Every step closer to her cell, Raven jumps and squirms in her binds. The wooden doors swing open, and he steps in.

She raises her head, eyeing him, waiting. Raven's wrists slip up into the shackles, and her hands grab the rusted chains. Roman approaches her then stands, with his arms folded over his chest, saying,
"Why did you do it? why did you set them up?"

Raven's fangs descend. Telling him to back off, but Roman grabs a flail and smacks her in the head. Raven's pretty face is thrown back, and she hisses at him.

Blood drips down her cheeks as droplets fall to the cold slab floor, rats rush to lap it up.

The flail is covered in her blood as it drips off the spikey ball trickling down the chain and wooden handle. Until her blood touches Roman's hands.

He drops the flail and picks up a rag, drying his hands.

Then throwing the rag on the torture table.

Roman begins to feel dizzy, he grabs his head, and doubles over. Rolling his neck back and forth. Then the visions start. His fangs descend, and his eyes begin to turn red, his skin becoming grey, and veins commence, protruding out all over his body.
 Raven watches in horror. As Roman becomes the devil personified. Hissing at him.

Men scatter out of the cell. Yelling, and pushing each other out of the way, and asking, "What the hell is that thing?"

But Roman grabs Raven, biting into her neck. She screams. Trying to fight him. She wiggles and squirms in Roman's grip, but his power is too great. And her binds too tight for her. Roman bites her again, taking chunks of flesh in his mouth till her head leans over her shoulders. Her eyes close. Death is upon her.

Roman's vision begins to show him events taking place. Upstairs in the castle. Belvidere blocks my bedroom door with silver in his hands. As the other Vampires want to taste my blood. I try sending Roman messages, but he doesn't receive them. I try to hide, but I know I'll be

Kiss Of Life

spotted quickly. I look for secret passages throughout my room but find nothing. I search for weapons, but I know I wouldn't be fast enough for them.

I could never beat them.
I hear the commotion outside my door, my heart pounds so fast, I feel like I can hear it, I know they do.
Shaking in my skin, I try one more time to get Roman's attention.

I put myself in a yoga position called, Sukhasana.
I get on the floor, sitting Indian Style, bring my fingers over my knees facing upwards.

I send Roman messages of help, asking him to pick up on my fear.

"Crying I tell him, help, I'm in trouble, come fast."

I choose to accept the inevitable. *If the others get through Belvidere, I'm dead.* I told myself.

I hear Belvidere, Screaming, "Get back! Move back!" they hiss and try to claw him. The Vampires move like spiders, sporadically making dance-like movements with their feet, their backs hunched over, back and forth they step.

Donna Tischner

Belvidere raises his silver chains, swinging at them; it hits one of the Vampires in his tooth, knocking it out.
The Vampire puts his hand to his mouth, seeing his tooth, he rushes Belvidere. Belvidere moves back, hitting the door. When finally, Roman approaches, wailing to get back or else. The Vampires retrieve back. Some still come at Belvidere, but Roman's powers kick in, he swings his arms, turning in a circle, from the wind the speed makes, sends everyone flying into walls, down the stairs and backwards on their bottoms. Roman tells them again, to back off. And they do.

As the other Vampires retrieve back to their rooms, Roman keeps getting more visions. This time, they become violent.

As the scenes play out in his mind, Roman collapses to the floor. Belvidere bangs on my door for me to open it. I hesitate, being scared. But Belvidere persists, "open the door!" I turn the knob and see Roman on the floor. We pull him into the room, getting him on the bed.
But Roman's visions aren't done with him yet.

Roman sits up on the bed, his eyes look forward, staring into the atmosphere. I wave my hand in front of his eyes,

Kiss Of Life

but he doesn't see me. Roman is quiet and still.

Belvidere and I look at each other, not knowing what to expect. Then Roman falls backwards onto the mattress.

Belvidere and I leave the room, letting Roman rest. But Roman's visions keep coming.
Roman regards his father and seven-year-old brother caught by the Ottoman diplomats.

Roman struggles to fight them. But their capture is horrific.

Roman's visions continue, and he sees them kill his father and little brother.

More visions come, Roman watches. The ottoman releases him after 5 years of being captured.

He remembers how he wanted his revenge. Orchestrating a dinner, he invites the Ottoman to come.

Then he has them slaughtered, piercing swords through their bottoms, and out of their mouths. He watches as they die slowly. Painfully.

Then he sits and eats his meal. As over 3000 men begin to

decline...
Roman screams violently as the visions play out. Wanting to forget his past and move forward to a new day. But his past haunts him, and he cannot let go.

Roman passes out. He sleeps for three days. Belvidere and I check on him often.
After Romans attacks, he begins to feel better. Not having other visions since his ordeal.

Roman greets me outside my bedroom door, walking us to breakfast. His arm entwined in mine as we go into the dining room.

As we sit, Roman notices some of his guests are no longer with us. Recalling at least 5 had their lives ended for various reasons.
The other Vampires watch as Roman sits sipping his drink during breakfast, wondering what has been going on with him. They start to inquire about what has happened and demanding answers.

I look at Roman shaking my head back and forth as if to say, *DON'T TELL THEM*! Roman hears my thoughts.

He places his hand on top of mine, telling me it will be

Kiss Of Life

alright.

Roman addresses his guest, saying, "I owe you nothing! Your demands are out of line! And you will never speak to me like that again!"

The others drop the conversation and continue with their meals. Roman smiles at me, and we leave the room.
By nightfall, Roman leads me outside on the Castle grounds to speak to me in private. He takes me to the end of the Cliff. Staring down at the rivers and Forrest. I begin to feel a little uneasy. Wondering why he's taken me to the Cliff. I feel my hands start to shake and look for something to grab onto. But there is nothing to hold other than the knee-length rock fence.

As the winds pick up, blowing my dress behind me and my hair flying all over, he places his hand on my shoulder, telling me,
"Your blood is very potent to me. You have seen what it does. I believe I had too much."

Roman turns his back to me, standing towards the fence. There's a pause from him. He walks a few steps then looks back at me, saying,

"I have seen the past. I have seen the present, and I have

Donna Tischner

seen the future.

 With your blood, I have powers to take out this entire City. I can take out hundreds of armies at one time."

I stand there listening, Not moving as the winds proceed to blow. Terrified out of my mind, I stand my ground. Roman turns back to me and states,
"There is nothing I can't do, you and me, together? We will be unstoppable!"

I swallow. Then I put my hand to my face rubbing my forehead. I cannot believe what I just heard from Roman.

Roman tells me, "Your thoughts are screaming at me! I can hear everything you conceive. Your heartbeat is racing so fast that you will make yourself ill if you don't slow it down.

There is no need to feel afraid or frightened of me. I'm not going to throw you over the Cliff. I would never hurt you; I plan to marry you soon.

And I know you think I am crazy, but I'm not."

I walk over to Roman as he speaks, standing face to face;

Kiss Of Life

I place both my hands on his cheeks, cupping them as he watches me, his mouth turning into a smile, asking him, "You plan to marry me?" He bends down and places a kiss on my lips. He tries to pull away, but I force him in for a deeper kiss. He laughs and holds me firmly. His kiss becoming more intense, I moan, and hold Roman, placing my hands around his back, and my face to his chest. He answers me,

"Yes Princess, I am going to marry you."

Roman and I saunter through the gardens, he grabs my hand, and he guides me to a door hidden in the Leyland Cypress-Hedges. I stop and pull him back to me, but he pulls me to enter the opening with him: I tell him I'm afraid, but he keeps pulling me, I pull him back again, then he says,

"I need to show you something. Come."

Donna Tischner

Chapter 11:
THE CHAMBERS

Hidden in the garden of hedges is a secret door. Dried grass and dead plants surround the territory. Roman opens the door.

I investigate the dark hallway. It feels cold. We step in, and Roman lights a candle.

I grab onto Romans Jacket. I'm scared. Roman takes my hand in his. He squeezes my fingers assuring me everything is okay.

He leads us down the dark corridor. I feel the dust getting caught in my lungs, and I cough.

I put my hand on the cold slab, feeling the walls. Spider webs line the halls, and centipedes scatter over my fingers. I scream from the feel of them running over my hand.

Kiss Of Life

It's damp and rugged. I can hear rats squeaking as we walk.

I feel the floor, a steep hill. We turn around the bend of the walls, and he stops.

Staring at a double set of closed doors. Splintered wood, chips and scratches, claw marks down the decorated wood panels. They told a story.

Huge ring handles, that rusted over the decades lay on broken hinges. And the doorknob, a rusty long handle.

Roman asks me to keep an open mind and not say a word when he opens the door. I stare at him, not knowing what to expect. Then he opens the doors.

I bend my head to the side, peeking into the room. My eyes open wide. I quickly put my hand to my mouth. I am trying to keep silent. I look back at Roman with a question in my eyes. But he leads me into the room. We stand there, I look deeper at what I'm seeing, and I don't like it.

I run out of the room and down the dark halls, not knowing where I am going, but I keep running. I find a door and open it. I go in and stand with my back to the door, breathing heavy. With my hand covering my face, I begin shaking my head back and forth.

I hear Roman's footsteps coming down the hall, and I run deeper into the room through another door. I don't know why I'm running from him, but I need to be alone for a few seconds to catch my breath and think.

I hear Roman call my name, but I don't answer. I feel the floor under my feet, I'm standing on something hard, it's too dark in the room, I kick things, as I walk making noise. Roman opens the door and lets the light in from his candle, when I look back at the floor, I see what I'm standing in. Diamonds, Brass, and Golden Ornaments that border the Slate. Roman calls me, "Jewel's." I move a little, and he tells me I shouldn't be in this room. But I can only respond to him, "What's the difference? I don't care about all these Jewels." Roman helps me over the many goods lying on the floor, and we leave the room.

I told Roman I want to leave this forsaken underground chamber.
But he asks me, "can I bring you back into that room without you losing it?" I nod my head.

But Roman grabs me and pushes me against the cold wall and begins to comfort me. I slide down against the wall

Kiss Of Life

holding my head crying from seeing that.

Roman kneels to me on the floor. Placing his hands on my knees saying, "I know what you feel, but you're the only one I can trust to help me in this situation.
I ask questions, and tell him, this is too much to handle. My heart aches.

But Roman assures me he is trying to do the right thing.

Then he leads us back down the hall.
We walk back to the double doors. I feel my hands shaking, and my heart begins to race; my knees knock as Roman holds me up. He leads us into the room.

"Roman. how do you expect me to help?"
"Princess, please just look again."

Turning and walking back out of the room, Roman is aware of my behavior as upset as I am. He runs after me; I walk faster down the corridor.
"Stop! Let me explain!"
Roman said.
I turn and stare at him. I feel my tears streaming down my face.

Roman attempts to hold me, but I try to pull away; he

grabs me tightly. I cry, asking him questions. I put my face to his shoulder, and Roman holds me rubbing the back of my hair.

"I don't understand; what is that? They look sick, cold, and hungry. They're dying."

"Yes. They are all those things. I need you to help them."
"Why are they in there?"

"Princess, try to understand. We need them; they are our suppliers. They give us their blood. They are ill."
"You feed on them? they allow this?"
"Yes. Can you help them?"
"Me? How can I help them? They need doctors, professional medical treatment."
"Tell me what you think they need, and I will get it for them."

Back in the chamber room, the many patrons sit on the cold floor. Some sick with fever and coughing up blood. Some with bad injuries need antibiotics and bandages. And some, shivering with chills.
Nilsa has a high fever, and Bobby is bleeding from his nose.
Nilsa tries to crawl over to Bobby to help him. But she can

Kiss Of Life

barely make it as she collapses in the middle of the floor.

Dirty water sit in corroded containers as William tries to clean his wounds with it.
Others can't move or talk from being so sick.

Rats scatter in and out from under the doors and bite the patrons leaving them sicker with disease.

They moan in agony and lay on the dirty concrete floor in their own feces.

They beg for their lives to be taken just to be free of their diseases. Wails of pain and sorrow echo through the chambers.

***

Roman and I talk about their needs. I stand looking at him. Patiently he waits for my answers. I begin to tell him my thoughts.

"First of all, get them off the floors. Second, they need medication, antibiotics. Clean bandages and clean water in clean containers! Give them clean beds and blankets to lay on, and fresh garments.
These people are helping you. You should be treating them better!

They need to be separated into different cells, at least temporarily, until we know for sure if their diseases are contagious.

Each cell should be scrubbed and sanitized from the germs. Those rats need to be caught.

Their diseases can infect you if you drink from their blood, and the other Vampires. I realize you have the capabilities of healing on your own, but you shouldn't take the chance even still.

They really need a doctor. I am not a doctor nor a nurse. But common sense tells me, they need medication.
They should be generously paid, for all they have been through.
You told me; they are here on their own free will. Give them the option, to stay or leave once they get better.

They need sunlight of some sought. And real food. 3 meals a day. You need them, and they need to be adequately treated."

Roman looks into my eyes as I stand there waiting for his thoughts on my advice. Then he says to me.

Kiss Of Life

"It is done! Everything you told me to do will be completed by the end of the week. You have done well, my Princess." Again, he said, in another language. "Printesa mea."

Back at the Castle, Roman and I prepare for dinner. After we dress, Roman leads us to the dining room, and we eat. Talking and sipping our wine and other select drinks, when Tamara, another Vampire begins to cough. She sips her glass again and continues to speak with the others.

As we sit back in our chairs, Tamara starts to cough again. Tapping on her chest, she questions herself about the cough, but it stops. Then starts again. This time she cannot get the cough under control.

Blood runs from her eyes, and she keels over. Wiping her face with her hands, she sees the blood, asking what's happening to me.

The others scatter away from her in horror and watch as she coughs and grabs her stomach. Chairs fall over, and dishes land on the floor. Roman and I stand. Looking at the last thing she ate, realizing it wasn't her meal.

Immediately I grab the containers of Plasma on the table,

having them poured out.

Roman grabs Tamara taking her into the dungeon away from everyone else. Unsure what's happening, he restrains her in ropes to the bed. Then Seeks a doctor for help.

Belvidere has all the Plasma removed from the house and then begins to worry the Vampires will want to feed on the only humans in the Castle. Talking with Roman, he tells him of his suspicions.

Roman has all the humans in the house sent away, except for me.

I worry too now that I am very vulnerable. But Roman keeps me in his room.

When the Vampires need to feed, it could get worse, and I fear for my life.

As the days go by, the need for them to feed becomes grave. I hear them at my door, pacing the floors and hissing. I hide under the blankets in Roman's room, waiting for this to pass. But they keep coming back, standing at the door waiting for me to leave the room.

Kiss Of Life

They call for me to come out, and scratch at the walls.

But Roman tells them to get back and threatens to take their heads.

They attempt to fight Roman, they're desperate. And will do whatever they need to do, to get to me.

Roman becomes deranged, in his anger to protect me, he fights one of the Vampires, and takes his head in one swift move. As the deceased Vampires blood drips down the walls, and splattered through-out the hallway floor, Roman reminds the others, this will be them too if they attempt to get at Jewel again.

The others scatter in fear back to their rooms.
The following week, Tamara makes progress, showing signs she is healing.

As a house doctor came in and revealed none of the sick were seriously ill. Some of the patrons in the hidden chambers did not have severe illnesses, either. They too, are showing signs of progress.

We Learned some had Hepatitis A. Which could have been a severe contagious disease. This disease affects the

liver. It is caused by having dirty water and food.
Tamara's eyes bled from breaking a blood vessel from coughing so much.

The patrons living conditions were made better, and they received beds, blankets, clean running water, and fresh food daily. They are much happier.

Roman pays a visit to all the patrons in the chambers. He rewards them with gold and other fine jewels as they requested for their families. Even though their families are not aware of their doings.

As the week's pass, all the other humans have been brought back into the

Castle. Tamara is back to being her old witty self. Laughing about the ordeal.

Roman and I finally get to have some quality time together, as he makes plans for us to have a romantic dinner for two on the veranda. Looking forward to it, we prepare to be together.

Chapter 12:
OUR TIME

Roman calls for me at my bedroom door. He is greeting me with fresh flowers. I open my door and see him standing with the bouquet in his hands. I smile sweetly, kiss him on his cheek and take the flowers, placing them in my room.

Roman enters my room and pours us drinks. Then he hands it to me, asking me if I would like to sit. We sit on the sofa, and he leans in for a delightful kiss.

I can already feel my body reacting to him. He smells sensational, he looks like royalty, and his behavior is above exceeding, sweeter than I've ever seen.

I smile at him, knowing he's reading my thoughts. Roman tells me, "I heard that." I smile, asking him if he'd like to go upstairs now.

He takes my hand and leads us upstairs to his room, and we stroll over to the veranda. Once there, he tells me how beautiful I look this evening. Pulling out a chair for me. I

sit.
Then Roman tells me he's been wanting to talk to me about something, and right away, I begin to think our night is going to be ruined.

When Roman smiles at me, saying, "I hope it's going to get better." I look at him with a wary glimpse. But he says to me, "Princess, you have nothing to worry about." He takes my hand in his, kissing it, then he kisses up my bare arm, kiss after kiss till he reaches my lips, Kissing them softly.
I'm intrigued. *What the hell is going on here.*

Again, Roman heard my thoughts, and he smiles at me.

The servants bring in our meals and place the napkins on our laps. I look up at the server, thinking, this is very strange, squinting my eyes and cracking a smile.

Roman and I eat. He watches me as I sip my wine and shift in my seat.

When finally, I've had enough, and I ask him, "what is going on?"

He stands, sliding his chair out from behind him. Then

Kiss Of Life

walks over to me and stands there. "Roman, what are you doing?" smiling. He takes my hand and pulls me to my feet.

The music playing in the background is.
No ordinary love. By Sade.
Roman asks me to dance.
How can I resist him? His charm and magnetism are enchanting.
Roman, I say, "You have beguiled me."

Smiling, he swirls me into his chest, moving back and forth to a slow one-two sidestep. Holding me close, my hand clasped in his, resting on his heart, he stares me in the eyes. Then dips me back and plants a gentle kiss on my mouth. Roman pulls me back up and gets on one knee, pulling a small, opened box from his pocket.

Gasping, I pull him to his feet and grab hold of him. Clutching him tightly.

Tears drip down my face; I kissed him with all the strength I have. A posh smile formed on his mouth, and then Roman said to me, "You are special; I had never felt this way for any woman, not even when I was mortal. I love you."

Donna Tischner

Roman slid the vast diamond on my finger.
Standing, I tell him, "Yes, I will marry you."

Roman takes me in his arms, carrying me to his bed. Lying me down, he slides on top of me, and begins kissing me, and holding me. His sincerity is paralyzing, and his passion is mesmerizing.

Roman gently removes my dress from my shoulders, kissing them. Swaying back and forth, kissing my neckline.

My fingers roam his hair as his hands slip down my thighs. I hear him breathing heavily as his movement begins to dance around my waist. Rejoicing in his captivity, under the ecstasy of his loving, I begin to undress Roman.

It doesn't take long before I feel him inside me. His hands roam my breasts. When he leans down and pinches over them with his fangs. I yelp in a touch of distress, but soon it is forgotten, and Roman continues to embrace my blood.

His hands wrap around my back, and he holds me tightly to his chest. Moaning, I watch him endeavor in our passion. I shift my hips in a swift movement grabbing Roman's arms. He watches me and waits for my cry in

Kiss Of Life

ecstasy. Raptured by the cry, Roman's delight sends him into a welcoming pleasure.

In the morning, he tells me how I am like a symphony that plays him like a violin repeatedly.

I smile, kissing his pretty face.
Then he says, " We will be celebrating our engagement this weekend, and the wedding will take place next month."

Smiling at Roman, I take his hand, kissing it.

At breakfast, *Roman makes the announcement that Jewel's and I will be married in one month. Prepare for our engagement this weekend.*

There are whispers at the table, talking and laughs.

Roman slams his fist down in anger on the table, vibrating all the dishes and glasses. Roman stands to his feet, reminding the others that they will respect him and leave if they disapprove. But soon, the other Vampires give us their approvals and apologize.

New excitement has transpired from them, and Tessa joins me in the arrangements. I have asked Tessa to be my maid of honor. She excepted.

With all the planning, three other ladies have asked to help. Rochelle, Lena, and Misty. I was happy to accept their offer of help and have made them Brides Maids.

Lena was a hairstylist and will be doing my hair for both occasions.

Rochelle was a seamstress and has asked to make both my Wedding Gown and Dress for my engagement party. Misty didn't have much to offer but just being there, which was good enough for me. And Tessa asked to arrange all the decorations.

We have been together every day since the announcement. The girls are really excited for us, and I feel honored.

Roman has asked Jimmy to be his best man. Jimmy has been Roman's friend for over 350 years. They have been through wars and other encounters together over that time.

Trevor, Scott, and Brian, too, have been with Roman for many years. They will act his ushers.

Kiss Of Life

Roman has arranged many guests for both parties. Our engagement party will have over 300 guests and over 300 for the Wedding.

The Castle will be terribly busy the next month.

As the weekend approaches, Rochelle has brought me my gown and an exquisite piece of work.

The color is powder blue with swirls of silver up and down the length. Puffy off the shoulder mid-length sleeves. A V line on the back that finishes just above the waist's edge. "It's perfect!" I said to her.

Lena has done my hair in an updo. A braid that wraps around my head and strands of hair fall on my face and around my neckline.

"Beautiful." I said to Lena.

Roman is wearing a black 3-piece suit.
His white puff shirt covers his neck. And his vest has silver sequences of leaves going down the buttons. Roman's Jacket is long, with a peaked lapel and more silver line the 3 buttons in front.

Donna Tischner

The Castle's Ball Room is ready with all its decorations and many guests that have come from various countries in celebration of this occasion.

Some of the guests wait anxiously to meet me. I am nervous about the introductions, as many are Vampires.

As the guest make their entrances, Roman waits outside my door for me to escort me downstairs. Our Bridal Party will be accompanying us.

Tessa opens my door. Roman's eyes fall upon my dress and then my hair.
A radiant smile forms on Roman's lips with great approval.

He speaks to me, saying, "I am so proud of you! Your beauty is above anything I have ever seen." Then he kisses me.

I feel so overwhelmed and want to cry; the girls realize and tell me how good I am doing. As Roman entwined his arm in mine, we proceed to the staircase.
Many guests stand at the bottom of the stairs, staring up as we come down.

Kiss Of Life

We reach the bottom of the steps, and we are flooded with guests kissing and hugging us. Roman keeps me tight to his side, protecting me from any possible danger. Soon we make our way to the Ball Room, and everyone applauds our entrance.

Walking hand in hand, we enter the Ballroom. The lighting is low, and the live band plays a saccharine slow ballad. Roman spins me, and I glide into his arms. He places a gentle kiss on my lips and begins swaying us to the melody. I inhaled deeply and kept my gaze on him as Roman swirls us around the floor. Stepping to the side and around gracefully, down the floor's length, he picks up the tempo, and then dips me, bringing us back together. Until the dance reaches a conclusion, and kisses me again on my lips, I curtsied to him and he bowed his head to me, soon walking back to our seats.

As Roman and I sit sipping our drinks, he begins to touch his head. Rubbing his temples and looking down. I realize something is wrong when he asks me to bring him to his room. We stand and nonchalantly leave the Ballroom.

The visions start again. This time Roman sees into the future. As a woman begins causing Havok on the party.

She throws a glass shattering it on the floor. Her long

Donna Tischner

Black hair covers her face, and her black gown spins around her legs as she moves swiftly across the room. Then stops at the arch of the door's threshold.

She holds onto the door jam, then laughs wickedly, letting her head dip back.

Roman whispers to me to go to my room and lock the door until he calls for me; I do as he says, I know he sees something unpleasant.

The woman calls out for me. Giggling and calling my name again. Roman falls to the floor, landing on his knees, grabbing his head in pain, leaning forward; he watches the vision play out.

The woman searches all the rooms for me on the first floor. Other Vampires try to stop her, telling her to get a hold of herself, but she bites into those trying to stop her.

When she finds me, smelling my fear, turns her on; she grabs me, throwing me to the floor and biting into my inner thigh, sucking, and draining my blood till there's nothing left but a skeleton.

Roman sees her face; in shock, he stands to his feet as the

Kiss Of Life

vision concluded. Running for the door and turning the knob, she's standing outside his door.

"Anne Shoemaker? Why are you up here?"
"Romanian, let me have her!"
""Who?"
"You know who, your little princess."
"Why?"
"I'm going to taste her and drain her; I'm doing you a favor."

Roman becomes unhinged. His face starts to distort, and his skin becoming grey, Anne watches in horror. Roman grabs her by her hair, in a swift move, she is flown across the hallway, hitting the wall. Anne stands ready to fight Roman.

His fangs descend, and his nails turn into claws as he swings at Anne, cutting through her like blades slicing wood. Anne bleeds, red blood pools out of her chest. Roman briskly aims for her, tossing her over his shoulder, Anne, hits the ground, in pain she whelps.

Anne stands, in her discombobulated state, speeding to get away from him. She jumps through a plane glass window, breaking it, and landing on her heels, fleeing the Castle.

But Roman is not satisfied as he goes after her. He looks through the trees and their limbs, searching the grounds, he finds her footprint. He follows them, leading Roman right to her.

He corners Anne in a dark patch of trees hanging by their branches.

She scurries, but Roman is right on her, digging his fangs into her throat, into her collar bone and ripping flesh from her chest. Hastily Roman stabs his knife-like claws into her heart. She becomes limp; Roman holds Anne as he brings her body to the ground.

Roman stands staring down at her beaten corps. He kicks dirt on her body in his brooding expression.
Then he picks her up and carries her deceased body back to the Castle, warning anyone who dare threatens to lay a hand on Jewel; this is how they'll end up. Roman drops Anne's body to the floor, showing them, he means business.

As the party comes to its end, Roman keeps me in my room, and he says his goodbyes to our guests.

Kiss Of Life

Once the house is empty of all the guests, Roman comes to see me.
He enters my room, walks over to me, then holds me tightly in his arms.

I look at his face, cupping my palm on his cheek, asking him if he is alright; he assures me he is fine.

I kiss him tenderly, explaining how sorry I am for all his friends who died on my account. But he stops me, saying, "This isn't your fault." He places his index finger on my lips, saying, "I don't want you to feel that way."

Roman takes my hand in his telling me to, "Come." We enter his bedroom, and he lays me down on his bed. Then he tells me, "I just want to hold you." Falling asleep.

In the morning, when I awake, Roman is not in the room with me. I get up and dress. Heading down to the Dining room. I see Belvidere asking, "Have you seen Romanian?" Belvidere tells me, "He's away on business."

I put my head down in sadness, taking my seat.

After breakfast, I sit in my room, waiting for Roman. But I don't see him.

Donna Tischner

Dinner passes, I still haven't seen Roman. Sadness takes over me. I'm missing him and unsure why he didn't mention he was going away. My mind begins to get the best of me; all these irrational thoughts come and go. Feeling disappointed, I go to sleep.
I wake in the middle of the night. In bed, with a headache and dizziness.
Not long after, I find myself in the bathroom vomiting. It's so violent I feel like death. I crawl back into my bed, wishing Roman were here with me. Then fall asleep.

In the morning, as I lay in bed feeling sick, thinking of Roman, the illness takes over me.
 Wanting to find Roman, I get off the bed, but I fall quickly to the floor. Trying to get up, I manage to grab the column and pull myself up. But I promptly fall again.

Passing out. On the bed's platform, lying there half on the steps and the floor.

Kiss Of Life

Chapter 13:
SICKNESS

Romanian's POV:

Finding Jewel on the floor passed out was scary. It has been three days, and she still hasn't woken up.

Belvidere has been placing cool cloths on her head, and her pressure points in hopes that her fever will drop.

I sit next to her on her bed, holding her hand and rubbing her face.

Her fever has gone up, so we have called in a doctor to look Jewel over.

I stay close to her as the Doctor does all her vitals. Then the Doctor places a I'V in her for fluids.

He takes her blood for further testing and tells me he'll be in touch as soon as the results are back.

I'm going out of my mind and feeling bad that I never told Jewel I was leaving for business last week. I didn't even say goodbye to her.
To make madders worse, Belvidere told me how upset she was and how she stayed in her room that whole day alone.

I have a bad feeling about this. I don't think Jewel is going to wake up. Whatever this disease is, it's killing her.

Tessa comes in every day talking to Jewel, Belvidere too and a few others.

I feel stinging in my eyes. I haven't cried in centuries. I believe I feel like that might happen. No one should see me, if that happens, it will be red tears. I leave Jewel's room briefly, going to my bedroom for a moment in my thoughts. That's when I felt them streaming down from my cheeks. I grab a cloth and dry my face, blood seeps through the fabric.

It's been six days. The Doctor finally calls me, saying he's coming over.

Kiss Of Life

He didn't mention if this was good news or bad. And I didn't ask. Feeling uneasy, in my ambiguous emotions, I don't ask.

When Dr. Collins walks into Jewel's bedroom, I can see the expression on his face; this is terrible news.

He reveals some news that I can't even fathom. Then he tells me how sorry he is. I guess that means this is farewell. And I won't accept it!

I kick everyone out of her room, yelling,
"Get out! Get out now!"

I lay next to Jewel on the bed crying, saying,
"No, this can't be happening!"
I pick up her limp body and watch as her arms dangle to the mattress, her head falling back; I cradle her in my arms. Sobbing in her chest, I see my own blood all over her. Then I begin speaking to her,

"Wake up, Princess, wake up for me! Please, please Princess."

I rub my face, smearing the blood on my cheeks, then leave, asking Dr. Collins, "What can we do? there must be something!" Dr. Collins looks at me in distress, shaking his head back and forth, apologizing to me, saying, "There is nothing further we can do. I'm sorry Romanian."

I go back to Jewel's side, sitting on the bed. I bite my wrist; blood seeps out; I put my wrist to her lips forcing Jewel to drink my blood. She manages to get a decent amount, swallowing it. Then I wait.

I turn down the lights, sitting on a chair near her bedside. Then I begin to wonder why I didn't see this situation in any of my visions. I realized it was because I hadn't had any of her blood in days. I might have seen this coming had I drank from her.
Feeling bad, I pick up her hand, holding it.

Four hours later, Jewel tries to speak. I jump to her side. Telling her, *I'm here*. She asks, *what happen*; when I tell her, *you have been poisoned and near death,* she attempts to sit up. I help her, propping some pillows behind her. Then I ask, "how are you feeling?" She begins to say; "I feel fine," when a sudden surge of energy strikes her body, jolting to her feet. I stand back. Watching as Jewel moves swiftly off the platform bed and to the door.

I yell, "Jewel, where are you going?"

Kiss Of Life

She tells me, "I need to run, I feel like I have all this energy, and I don't know why!"
"Wait, I'll come with you."

She stands at the door, asking, what is going on with me? I tell her to come back and sit, but she is too apprehensive and can't sit still.

Then she starts asking me questions.

"Who poisoned me, and what was it?"
"I haven't investigated that yet, but plan to, and the poison was Cyanide."

"Well, why do I have all this sudden energy?"
"Princess, sit. We need to talk."

Jewel's face is undecipherable. Her hair swings back as she moves vigorously through the room. She convenes on her bed and waits for me to finish. I take her hands in mine. Rubbing my thumb over the tops of her hands. I look Jewel in the eyes and then say to her,

"You were dying! I had to give you my blood to bring you back to me! I couldn't go on without you!"
"I drank your blood?"
"Yes."

Donna Tischner

"Am I a Vampire?"
"No. You are not."

Jewel cups her hands to my cheeks and places a long, sweet kiss on my lips. I study her as she looks at me with tender eyes.

"Roman, you couldn't live without me? Really?"
"Princess, I was out of my mind. I was scared and desperate."

"Roman, I'm not mad, you did what you had to do. I understand."

I couldn't help but grab her and hug her so hard she began to laugh, saying, "I can't breathe."
I hugged her too tight, apparently.

Jewel's showers and tells me she'll be down for dinner soon. I tell her not to worry about the meal; I will be inspecting the kitchen.

Once I get down to the kitchen, I begin to search for the poison. No one in the Castle knew Jewel was poisoned. We kept everything secret. Afraid we would scare off a potential murderer.

Kiss Of Life

When I walk into the kitchen, all the cooks and server's freeze. They begin to rush me, asking if they can get me anything. But I tell them to continue with their duties.

I need to know who it was and why someone here wants Jewel dead. I look through the cupboards and the walk-in freezer; I checked out the pots and pans, all the stored foods, and even under the sink. But I find nothing.

I decide it's time to talk to Jewel. I make my way back upstairs to her asking her if I can taste her blood. I need to see it in a vision. With-out her blood, I can't see it.

I ask, and she bends her neck to the side.
Jewel tilted her head without question or argument. Not one word was spoken of it.

I kiss her all over her face and down her neck. Then biting into her, taking in her sweet blood. She moans. Romantically.

We waited in Jewel's room until the vision came on. When suddenly, it plays out like I'm with the would-be killer.

She takes the Cyanide, pours it over Jewel's dish. Then

brings it into the dining room as Jewel awaits her breakfast. I cannot make out this person's face.

Her head is covered when Jewel asks her to remove the hood from her hair.

The lady reluctantly brings the hood to her shoulders and gives Jewel an irritated face. But Jewel doesn't like that she was disrespectful and asked her if there's a problem; the woman says no and attempts to leave the room. Now, the other Vampires at the table notice how disrespectful she was; asking her name, she tells them, Alicia. Then they make her apologize to Jewel.

The vision plays out in much detail, but my head can't handle it; I fall on my knees, holding my head. Jewel grabs me, telling me to stop looking into the vision. As she was saying that I see more.

Alicia's long dark hair falls on her shoulders, and she swings it over her collar, walking out of the dining room. I watch as Jewel takes a bite of her scrambled eggs. Then she sips her juice. Jewel finishes all her breakfast. Then Alicia comes back in and takes her dish.

She tells her friend Vivian, another server in the kitchen,

Kiss Of Life

how in love she is with someone in the Castle. Vivian asks who, and she tells her,
 "Sir Romanian." Vivian tells her not to let anyone hear her speaking like that. And she leaves the kitchen.

But Alicia tells her friend, I'm going to make him mine! Vivian tells Alicia, you're going to end up dead; watch yourself.

I finally sit up, staring into Jewel's eyes and saying, "I've got her!"
I asked Jewel to wait up here for me while I deal with Alicia.

I run down the steps finding some reinforcements to take with me. I make my men stand behind me. As we enter the kitchen, Alicia is setting up our plates. I see the Cyanide in her pocket.

I walk over to her and grab her wrist. Alicia is shocked, she gasps, I hear her heart pounding in her chest. Then pick her up by her throat, throwing her across the room. She hits the countertop and falls brutally to the floor. I watch as she tries to get up and then slips back down. Then I grab her again in one hand, holding her in the air, her feet dangle.

Donna Tischner

She's choking under my hand.
Her face is turning red. Her eyes tear up.

Then I let her go, falling to the floor, yelling, "Alicia, how could you do that? You have no idea what love is."

 Alicia cries, begging me to forgive her. And asking if Vivian gave her up. I grab her again, squeezing her throat, then I pull the Cyanide out of her pocket. I tell my men to bring her to the dungeon.

The other servers watched in horror; I tell them, to get this food clean up and sterilize the dishes and bring us in fresh plates.

 Then Vivian approaches me, saying, "She told me she is in love with you; I had no idea of her plot. I'm sorry, Sir Romanian." I responded, "You should have come to me regardless." I walked away.

Early in the morning, Jewel wakes before I; she begins kissing me, stroking the hair off my face. I growled when she climbed onto me, moving her hips about my waist, and kissing my neck, rubbing her hands over my chest, and moaning. I flip her over in one passionate move. She smiles at me, saying, "Well?" I grab her hands, pinning

Kiss Of Life

them over her head and subduing her. She laughs wickedly.

She begs me to release her hands, but I tell her no. She says she needs to touch me; her eyes are soft and enticing. I release them, and she grabs me by my waist, pulling me closer to her, saying, "I can't get enough of you! I need to have you now!"

Just hearing that, I begin to move spontaneously over Jewel. Her erotica is enticing and alluring me. Concluding, I hold her, cradling Jewel in my arms.

Later, Jewel tells me she needs to go home to the States. But I tell her, soon we will go back. I watch as her face becomes tense, and saying in a sharp voice, "NO, NOW WE GO!"

She grabs me by my hand, and then she falls to the floor. I try to pick her up, but she becomes feisty, holding my hand again, her face becomes white. She looks up at me angrily, her eyebrows meet in the middle, and her mouth bends down with a frown.

She stands to her feet and begins to speak, saying, "You lied to me? You went to the States without me? How could you do that?"

Donna Tischner

I'm unsure what's happening and shocked.

Jewel then says, "You knew I needed to get home, but you went ahead without me anyway? I don't understand how you could do that?"

She reaches her hands to hit me, but when Jewel's hand touches mine, I get zapped across the room, slamming the dresser. She comes at me again, zapping me more and with more force. She tells me to stay on the floor and not to get up. She leaves the room, running down the stairs out the front door.

I stand there in shock, then run after her, but she's gone. I yell to Belvidere, "Find my fiancé! Now! and bring her back to me!"

Later in the evening, Belvidere came to me saying, "She boarded a plane for the USA, two hours ago." I yell to get the Jet ready, taking Tessa, Trevor, and Belvidere, with me back to the States.

***

Jewel's POV:

Kiss Of Life

As I make my way down the long steep hills of the Castle grounds, brushing through the trees and their limbs, I find myself developing agility I didn't know I have.

I run without looking back. I know if Roman is near, he'll slow me down. I keep going till I see the tall metal fence; as I approach it, I leap into the air jumping over it, and landing on the road.

I find my way into a town and look for a phone. But I can't find one. I ask a gentleman if he can tell me where the US Embassy is, and he points, across the street. Surprised, I run to the embassy asking for help.

Once they let me in, and I explain, an unknown man kidnaped me.

They question who the man is, asking if I know where he took me to and if I have, ID. But I tell them, the man has my purse, and I have no idea where I was. I felt like I was being interrogated for hours when finally, they put me on a plane back to the USA.

Nine hours later, we're landing at the airport. I ask to use the ticket desk phone and call Brook to come and get me.

Donna Tischner

Once I see Brook, I break down, hysterically crying. She holds me warmly, saying, "It's okay now; your home and safe." I tell her to take me home to my house. Brook stays with me for the night. In the morning, she leaves for work.

Now I'm alone in my parent's house, and I have time to think about everything I have been through this past month. Reflecting, I realize how I loathed most of those Vampires in Romania.

I walk through the house, checking everything out. I go into my parent's bedroom and sit on their bed, thinking about the day we found Jeremy in the closet. I decide to go into the closet and look.

I get close to the door, put my hand to the doorknob, and I get jolted. I fall to the floor; with my hand still on the doorknob, I begin to see a vision.

My parents are talking near the closet in their room; my mother tells my father she has seen some unusual things here in town. My father questions her about what she saw. She tells him she saw a man carrying a body to a wooded area. Then he asks her if the man saw her, she replies, she is unsure.

Kiss Of Life

I drop my hand off the doorknob and remained on the floor. Thinking to myself, what the hell is happening to me?
I stand to my feet and touch the knob again, being zapped and falling to the floor. Another vision plays out.
My mother is getting into her car. It's late and dark outside. A man creeps up on her; she gets startled. She asks, "Can I help you?" but the man doesn't say anything. He grabs her and carries her to that wooded area.

Jeremy puts her down in the leaves. She's shaking, and tears fall from her eyes. Jeremy tells her not to be frightened, "I'm not going to hurt you."
He tells my mother Lynn, she is so beautiful, and he is highly attracted to her. Then he says that I have been watching you. He leans into Lynn, his lips just a kiss away from hers. She begins to relax, and Jeremy kisses her softly on her mouth.

She asks, "What are you?" But Jeremy doesn't want to answer. Then she asked, "How is it that you can fly?" Jeremy tells her, "I am a man of many traits, and you will be safe if you are with me." He holds my mother in his arms, saying, "We should be together." But she told him she is married. He kisses her again, then flies off into the night.

Donna Tischner

This meeting of the hearts went on for years. The two would be together when they could. They started to develop feelings for one another; Jeremy even told her he was in love with my mother. After sleeping together, she found that she was in love with Jeremy. But she couldn't end her marriage.

Jeremy was not happy with that, and they began to fight over it.

Lynn had given birth to a baby girl. Later Jeremy found she had a baby and was hurt over her secret pregnancy.
One night, they agree to meet one last time; Jeremy puts her down in the leaves. She's hurt by their relationship ending, and tears fall from her eyes. Skid drops out of a tree, landing on her back. Jeremy bites her on the leg, and Skid bites into her collarbone.

My father is looking for my mother; then he yells out, calling her name, Jeremy and Skid scurry off. She cries out, my father finds her. She is bleeding to death. He picks her up, rushing back to the house. My father lays my mother on their bed.

Mom is declining. My father screams in pain. My mother

Kiss Of Life

tells him, "Let me go." He yells, " No! I can't. I'm going to kill them!" Still crying to my mother, "Hang on baby." But again, she tells him, "Please let me go." He grabs my mother holding her, as she bleeds, saying how much he loves her. Mother passes in my father's arms. He cradles her, sobbing.

When my father puts her down on the bed, Romanian is standing in front of him. My father is startled. He asks, who are you and why are you in my house. Romanian tells him, "I'm sorry about your wife.

But we need to fix it, so no one knows how she passed." Dad stands charging Romanian, but Romanian stops him. Telling my father, "No one can know about this, us. I need to use my blood to fix the wounds."

My father asks him, "Are you, their leader?" Romanian replies, "Yes."

Romanian walks over to my mother, placing his blood on her bite wounds, making them disappear. Then he tells my father, "You will have a Funeral for your wife and tell your daughter she died from pneumonia." My father beckons him and asks, "How do you know about my daughter?"

He replies, "I've been watching her since her birth. I know

everything about her." My dad comes at him again, saying, "You will stay away from my daughter! I'll kill you if you lay one hand on her!" But Romanian tells him, "I have no intentions of hurting her; she will be safe as long as I am around."

"Why have you been watching my daughter?"
"She is special."
"In what way?"
"Her blood is rare; she has special abilities."
"What abilities?"
"That is of no consequence, enough questions."
My father shows Romanian to the door.
After the vision ended, I sat on the floor crying. I cried so much; I fell asleep near their closet.

The next day I awake on the floor, my eyes open, and I lie there for some time before getting up to shower.

 Once I get dressed, I look out the window at Roman's house. It seems quiet there, so I go about my business.

***

Romanian's POV.

Kiss Of Life

After Jewel left the Castle, I went down to the dungeon to deal with that psychopath, Alicia.

She had been bound to the torture table and gagged. I know she heard me coming because she had peed herself right down to the floor when I got in her cell.

The doors swung open, and I could hear her heart racing; I enjoyed her being so frightened out of her mind, she tried to break free of her binds. I told her to relax, and Alicia looked up at me with her big brown eyes. I removed the gag from her mouth.

Then asked her, "Are you frightened?" she replied, "Very!"

"Good!" I told her.
Then she asked me if I was going to kill her. I didn't respond.

I told her she tried to kill my Fiancé, and that is not acceptable. She apologizes over and over to me. But I'm not satisfied. I told her she doesn't deserve to live. There is no justice for what you have done.

I picked up a curved blade; it fit perfectly around her neck. She voided herself. She cries, begging me not to take her life. I took the curved knife away and threw it across the room.

Then a dish of food is brought in for her to eat.

I untied her, telling Alicia to eat. She asked if it was poisoned.

"Eat!" I said to her."
Crying, she begins to eat the food placed in front of her.

I waited till she ate every drop on the plate.

Then I chained her back to the table. Her hands over her head and her feet in shackles.

I watched as she begins to vomit, laying down and choking on it. Not long after, she coughs and retches more. I said to her, "How are you feeling? Do you like Cyanide? It feels good, doesn't it?"

Hour's pass, and then another dish of food is brought in for her again. Untying her, I make her eat more. She begs me not to make her eat anymore, but I push her on her

Kiss Of Life

shoulder, to the table to eat. Pushing her to sit down. She gags vomits and coughs. Then Alicia keels over and falls to the floor.

That'll teach you never to fuck with my family and me. Alicia's eyes stay fixed on Romanian, wide open, she dies.

Boarding the Jet, the next day, we make our way to the States.

Jewel has been feeling the strength of my blood and is now out of control. I have seen firsthand what she can become.

I knew I love this one.

Donna Tischner

Chapter 14:
UNCONDITIONALLY

After I showered, I had a million questions for Roman. I need to see him, but I felt betrayed. As my eyes burn from crying, I drive to town. I stopped in at the corner store and purchased some eyedrops and headache relievers.

Seeing many people laughing and enjoying themselves made me feel like I'm missing out on so much. I know I'll never escape Roman. He'd never allow me to leave him, especially now that we're engaged.

I love him, he means a lot to me, but this Vampirism is a hard life to live.

He's going to want to live in Romania.

As I drive back home with the sun setting, I know Roman will be up looking for me. Maybe I should go to him at the Victorian.

Kiss Of Life

I pull up in the driveway, grab my bags and walk to Roman's house.

Belvidere opens the door, greeting me with a kiss on my cheek. He tells me Romanian is in his room.

I walk up the stairs to Roman's room and knock on the door. He opens it and stands there staring at me. His look is disappointing, unapproving, and cold.

Before he can say anything, I tell him, "I'm sorry Roman, I had some visions myself. They were ungracious. You were in the images.

 I was mortified. I needed to be alone. I needed time to think.

Roman is quiet. Still staring at me.
"Say something."

Roman walks away and pours himself a drink, standing with the glass in his hand; he turns to me and says,
"I have nothing to say to you."

I stood there feeling like I was going to cry when he said that. I didn't know what else to do to get a response from him, so I said, "Fine, then I guess this is goodbye."

I took off my ring and placed it on his table, leaving the room to go home. As I am walking out his bedroom door, he reads my thoughts. Then he says to me,
"I know you love me."

I stopped. Turned to him. But Roman had nothing else to say to me. My spontaneous move taking off my ring, backfired.

I continued out the door and down the stairs, walking out the front door.

After I got in my house, I put on some music. I ponder in my thoughts about my father, how he knew about Roman. He knew a Vampire bit my mother. And Roman knew it was Skid and Jeremy the whole time. How dishonest he was to me. I cannot comprehend.

He even knew about my blood and my birth. *"And I'm the one apologizing?"*

I decide to call Brook and take her out to a club. I need to be around human people and drink my troubles away. Brook tells me she'll meet me at the club. I get dressed

Kiss Of Life

and go.

I meet Brook at the doors, and we go into the club together, going to the bar for drinks, then finding a table. I spot a few people, I recognized them. Tessa and Trevor. They see me. They come strolling over.

Tessa immediately kisses me, saying, "I'm so happy to see you!" I return the kisses saying, "It's nice to see you too!" I introduce them to Brook.

 Tessa and Trevor sit with us. We talked for a while, and then Roman regards me, walking over to our table.

"You look so beautiful Jewel."
"Thank you."
"Dance with me?"
He puts his hand out to me, taking it in his; we saunter to the dance floor.

No words are spoken between Roman and me; the silence is unbearable. The dance is slow and romantic. But my heart aches for him. I know he hears my thoughts. The only thing on my mind as we dance was, what's happening?

My head falls to Roman's chest, and I feel the tears

building up. Roman holds me on the dance floor, rocking back and forth.

A sweet melody plays on. I tell him telepathically; I will always love you.
There is no return affection from him.

The dance ends, and I leave, proceeding back to my table. Roman goes in the other direction.

Not long after, a gentleman asks me to dance; I look to see where Roman is because I know he would disapprove of me dancing with another man. But this guy is human, good-looking, and sophisticated.

I tell him yes. He leads us onto the dance floor, and it happened to be another slow song. Roman notices. Stands. Then he approaches us.

I watch as he gets closer to me, when Roman taps the man on his shoulder, telling him, "she's engaged to me; beat it!"

I look at Roman saying, "Not anymore, remember?" The man says, "I don't want any trouble." Then he leaves, thanking me for the dance.

Kiss Of Life

I look at Roman with squinted eyes questioning him, "Why did you do that? You said nothing to me; you expect me to be engaged to you? but you're treating me terribly."

Roman holds my upper arms. He keeps me there on the dance floor with him. Staring at me and not saying a word. I tell him, "Let me go; what is it with you? What's your problem?"

He does the unthinkable. Grabbing me and pulling me into a secluded room. I yell at him to let me go, but he won't. He rushes me into a dim-lit room, then grabs me, kissing me. I pull away, but he brings me back into his arms, his lips caressing mine. I fight him some more. Still, Roman doesn't let me go. I give into his kiss. I wrapped my arms around his neck.

Roman's hands grace my bottom as his lips seek out my throat. Kissing me more, when I moaned, he pushed me up against a table, lifting my dress over my thighs. His hips, swirling around mine. Roman feels my tears on his cheeks; he looks at me, asking, "Why are you crying?"

Thinking to myself, that's the first thing you said to me since before we danced.

Donna Tischner

But I answered him, saying,

"Because I love you, and you're treating me poorly."

Roman stares at me then says,

"I was hurt; you are the first woman I let into my life, told my secrets to, gave you more than any other, then you left me."

"Roman, you lied to me; you knew I needed to get home, you went ahead without me. I was hurt too! You are the first man I know I unconditionally love; I saw too much in my visions. I was deceived by you. I hate us being apart, but I don't want to live the rest of my life in Romania either."

"You belong to me! Remember that! No one can look at you; no one can dance with you! You're mine. You know Romania is my home; that is where we will live."

I turn my back to Roman, but he spins me to face him. I lean my bottom against the table than say,

"I won't live there. I'm sorry. I can't.
That's your home, not mine."

Kiss Of Life

"It will be your home too. You shall see. I won't take no for an answer."
"You don't have a choice, I won't go."
"Be very careful Princess."
"You're threatening me?"
"I make no threats."

"Really... I believe you're giving me no options, and that isn't fair to me. Release me from this relationship. Tell me goodbye then. I don't like the way you're treating me!"

"I already told you, you're mine, and you will be coming back with me to Romania in a few days."

I move away from Roman. Feeling appalled, I look at him with weary eyes.

He saunters over to me, taking my hand in his and bringing my fingers to his lips; he takes my fingers one by one and puts them in his mouth, sucking them.

Then he tells me to come home. Feeling like I have no choice, I go back to Roman's house with him.

Once back at the Victorian, Roman tells me he needs to be alone for the evening, and that I should sleep in my room. Shaking my head back and forth, I leave.

Changing for bed, I put on a black Camisole, pour myself some wine, then turn on my stereo playing some soft jazz, turn down the lights, and then sitting on the sofa.
I sip my wine slowly, listening to the winds picking up. It howls like a wolf. Feeling uneasy, I pull my drapes closed. Thinking about the storm brewing.

After some time, I go down to the kitchen to find something to eat. No one is around. I pulled out a bag of chips, began to eat them walking down the corridor, and opened a door, stepping in. It's Roman's office.

 Realizing, I shouldn't be in here, but I go in anyway. I turn on the lights, looking at the photographs on the wall.

I'm thinking, *A picture tells a thousand words, it's true.*

Staring, at a photo of Roman in his younger days. He's so good-looking. Tall and muscular. Roman is still sexy and good-looking.

Then I turn around facing his desk. I saw some documents and picked one up reading it.
The Vampires that died, between here and Romania,

Kiss Of Life

were mentioned in that document. And the reasons they died. Mentioned on all five occasions, was my name...

I felt sad for a moment putting the papers back down when Roman stepped into his office, asking why I'm in here.

I got startled, jumped back, and hit the wall, causing an elegant female statue to fall, catching it before it hit the floor.

I put the figure back, and Roman says,

" That statue is over 500 years old.
You shouldn't be in here. Now tell me, why are you in my office?"
'I don't know."
"You don't know?"
"I was curious what this room was."
"You know, curiosity killed the cat, right? Get out!"

Without saying a word, I left his office and went right to my room.

I closed my door, and sat on the edge of my bed, thinking about how rude Roman is, and his behavior and forwardness towards me, his condescending words could

Donna Tischner

use some subtlety to say the least.

I begin to get flustered, madder, and madder the more I think about him. I've had enough, I thought to myself. Leaving my room and walking up to Roman's room, I pushed open his door and told him,

"This has gone far enough! I'm sick of how you treat me, the way you talk to me, it's just rude, I may be mortal, but that doesn't give you the right to treat me the way you do! If you want to end my life, then just do it because I'm done being treated this way!"

Roman grabs me by my arm and then says,
"Get out before I finish you for good!"

Before I can say another word, he's pushing me through the door. Then he slams it. I stand there, bang on his door, then fall to the floor. Sitting there, I ended up falling asleep.

In the morning, Romans sees me on the floor in his hall. He steps over me and keeps walking.

I heard his door shut, waking me. I see him going down the stairs like he didn't even care I was on the floor

Kiss Of Life

sleeping all night. I sat there, my back against the wall and my knees up at my chin, putting my head down into my knees. I stayed there till Roman came looking for me to come to breakfast.

He's carrying a dress for me that he must have pulled out of my closet; he throws it at me, landing at my feet. He tells me to get dressed right now and meet him in the dining room.

I stand holding the dress between my fingers and go to my room, changing for breakfast. Once there, I sit. Never speaking one word to Roman. And he, not to me.

After, I stayed in my room till dinner.

By dinner time, I decided to leave the Victorian. I walked down the stairs and right to the front door, opening it and walking across the street to my house, wondering why Roman didn't try to stop me; I keep going.

I called Brook and a few other friends to come over. Thinking I'll have a get-together with them. I put the music on, turning it way up. I took out some chips and drinks. Before I knew it, I had a party going on in my home.

Donna Tischner

Laughing and drinking, Brook asked me to dance; we began dancing and laughing until Roman walked in. Grabbing me by my arm, a friend of ours, *Jack*, tried to stop him, placing his hand on Roman's shoulder. Roman turned to him, and his eyes turned red. Telling Jack to back away.

I yelled at Roman to let me go, but he gripped my arm tighter, flinging me to the front door, forcing me outside. I stepped onto my lawn, and he began yelling at me and pointing his finger in my face, then shoving me backward. I felt my body heating up. I felt my head start to spin. I had, had enough. My body started to tingle, and I put my hand to Roman's face zapping him back a few yards. I came at him with the agility of a Black Panther, zapping him again.

Roman falls to the ground, leaning on his elbow and his legs stretched out, putting his hands up to protect himself. He stands facing me, brushing himself off, telling me to do what you want, and walks away, going back to the Victorian.

The party went on all night, some falling asleep on my sofa, others on the rug. I went into my bedroom, closed my door, and locked it. I took off my jeans putting on a pink teddy. I drew the drapes closed. Then I turned towards my bed and lifted my blankets, sliding under them.

I lay there thinking of Roman, twisting and turning, until I felt my eyes getting heavy. I fought to stay awake but couldn't. I fell asleep.

I woke in the middle of the night. *Roman is standing in front of my bed, with his arms crossed over his chest. I called his name. "Roman?"*

He didn't say a word. Roman just stood there staring at me as I slept. I wondered how long he was there.

Then he put his hand out to me. Putting my hand out to him, he leaned in on the bed and kissed me.

I lifted the blankets for him to come in, tilted my head, and Roman began kissing my throat. Before I knew it, he was on top of me.

His kisses were complex, abrupt, and commanding. In the dark room, I could see his eyes changing. They became red with terror. I felt his skin becoming callus, his bones protruding. I heard groans of anger, and his grip tightened on me.

Donna Tischner

He ripped off my teddy, undressed himself, then slid into me in one sudden move. Painfully I yelp. He moved on top of me, swirling his hips and screeching like a wild animal. His hand on either side of me, holding himself up as he moved in and out. I was horrified. Then he bent down and bit into my neck; blood and tears dripped onto my shoulders. Again, he bit me over my breast.

Then again. Until I could no longer keep my eyes open, the blackness was too great. Death was upon me.

I jumped up so fast. Oh my God, it was a dream. Or was it?

Kiss Of Life

Chapter 15:
ROMAN'S STORY

At age 10, I learned quickly that the towners respected my father. They would greet him with the utmost admiration. Catering to him just out of fondness.

I was told one day I would be the next King. Although it didn't matter to me, I followed the rules and learned about a King's obligations.

I went about my business daily, not caring about what was going on around me. Playing as an average child would. But I was far from an ordinary child. I was a Prince...

When my mother gave birth to my two younger brothers years later, I became more aware of my responsibilities. Having had some duties on taking care of my two younger brothers.

Living in a Castle had its ups and downs. Our subjects were eager to assist when called upon, which was not often. Nevertheless, the Villagers were there for us if we needed them.

Later, when the wars broke out, my father took my younger brother, *Radu,* and myself to fight the Otterman diplomats. When they took all three of us hostage, subduing us in a cold cell.

After some time, they set my father and brother free in an agreement to keep me. They brutally beat my brother, blinding him and then burying him alive. I felt helpless in his capture, and my heart began to harden. My father was murdered too behind our home.

During my imprisonment by the Ottoman Diplomats, they gave me lessons in science, philosophy, and the art of war. Finally, they set me free after five years.

I was now King and had obligations to my Village and its people.

I vowed to kill every last one of my Captors at the time of my release. I orchestrated my armies and had special weapons made up.

I sought out a few psychopathic men in my Village,

Kiss Of Life

seeking their advice on brutal torture methods. Life was about to get better for my people. They would be free of their cruel diplomats.

I went into the mountains for days, gathering my thoughts, and would sleep under the leaves. Drink from the streams and eat whatever animals I could find. I needed that time to put everything together collectively.

Three days after, I decided it was time to return to my Village; I was then attacked and bitten by some animal I had never seen before.

It looked almost human, with ears that pointed up over his head. His mouth looked as if it had been bitten, missing a part of his upper lip. And teeth of pointed blades, designed to rip apart any prey.

His eyes were red, like fire penetrating me. He walked on two legs with arms that hung down to the dirt, almost like an Ape. He bit into my leg three times and then into my arm. The pain was unbearable, undeniable, and like venom bleeding into my bloodstream. I imagined he was enjoying my flesh and blood.

 I tried to grab the son of a bitch and fling him over my back, but his strength was of 100 Elephants.

Donna Tischner

I lay there in the leaves bleeding, dying. This creature dragged me off into a hole in the ground. I wanted to fight the beast, but I couldn't. I let him drag me down into the soil.

I went through some strange transformation. My body was reforming, becoming like that creature. After days, I awoke. My form was like a devil.

My skin color was grey. My eyes blood red and my teeth had formed fangs whenever I needed blood to drink.

Yet I looked human when my body was satisfied.

The sunlight was like fire burning me. I learned quickly that I could no longer be outside in the daytime.

I hid in that hole in the ground until that creature came back. I was furious at what I had become. I pierced my eyes into his soul and bit into him, draining him of all his blood. Then I threw his body out of the hole. Burning it.

By nightfall, I needed to feed more. I sought out bigger animals.

Kiss Of Life

Draining them. Before I knew it, I had the strength of over 1000 Elephants, myself, and the agility, of a cheetah chasing down its prey, only I was much faster.

My vision became magnified. I could see for miles upon miles. I had the hearing capacity to hear a pin drop. Or the most diminutive creatures walking in the forest. It took some time to adjust to this new body, but I was fierce, angry, and ready. I was fast, powerful, and unstoppable.

I needed to learn how to walk in the daytime, so I experimented with soils and different stones. When I learned, Tungsten was one stone that could withstand any element. I carried pieces of it in my pockets, allowing me to walk in the day. I was satisfied.

After returning to my Village, I was eager to get this war over with and live out my days as I was. Defending my Throne and Villagers was all I cared about at the time.

My impalement to the Saxon merchants, in Kronstadt was once allied with the Boyars, and was impaled for the murders of my family.
I thanked the Turks for my new nickname, kaziklu bey, meaning, "Impaling prince."
Not the best name, but they feared me, and with a name like that, they knew I meant business.

Donna Tischner

Once the war was over, I returned to my Castle, seeking out my wife to be. After meeting Justina, I felt as if life could go on to some normalcy.

I would never have children. My family name would end with me.

Decades passed, and I became weary of my time left on earth. Not having a family. I vowed women out of my life after my wife Justina cheated on me with my best friend. Searching for only one woman with extraordinary blood.

When I met Belvidere Weatherstone, in Romania, he agreed to become my personal live in Butler. He knew all my secrets and kept them to himself. Belvidere became a companion to my Estate and me.

He searched out every hospital in the USA for that special blood. The one who would give me more power and more diversity. The hospital was located in a small town in Upstate, NY. The baby was born, a little girl.

We watched her grow into a woman.
She is beautiful, intelligent, and talented.

Kiss Of Life

Her blood type is rare. She has powers I don't even think she's aware of, due to her rare blood. We attained knowledge of this baby 25 years ago. Learning her mother had been bitten by a Vampire but was never turned. The one who bit her, his blood lay dormant until she conceived.

We purchased a house on the same street as baby Jewel five years ago, a prominent Victorian. She was leaving for College in Manhattan when we were moving in. After her parent's deaths, she came home to take care of their family house—a quaint home.

Now Jewel has discovered her newfound powers, and she can be severely dangerous.

Belvidere sought out explanations on Jewel's rare blood, learning,
My blood combined with her blood created an overload of electrons. Enabling her to generate a force of electricity to flow from her body.

My blood activated these electrons in Jewel, resulting in igniting her abilities.

I have fallen in love with her and want her to become my wife. She is stubborn. She has standards. Values. And mortality.

I hadn't planned on falling in love, but this girl is unlike any I have ever met before.

I needed her blood. I came to her in her dreams. I knew she knew; they weren't dreams. After some time, she figured it out.

Her blood is like gold, flowing through a river. Only, the river is my veins.

 Making me stronger. Faster, and giving me the Visions to see the past, present and the future.

With her blood, I am God...
After I took her to Romania with me, my love for her had gotten stronger. But I still couldn't let her know that. I planned to keep feeding on her. Not falling in love.

Jewel fell in love with me too fast. I couldn't help but hear her every thought. After feeding on her, I would know wherever she was.

If she was in the dining room, I knew; if she flew home to

Kiss Of Life

the USA, I knew. It didn't matter; I will always know of her whereabouts.

Now my love has intensified, and I don't want to hurt her anymore. I want her to live a traditional lifestyle and have children.

 I cannot give her that. She deserves it.
I had let Jewel down. Deceived her.
Lied to her. And even beat her.
Yet, she still wants to be with me.

Trying to understand her love for me is like trying to figure out a Diophantine math equation. She's that complex.

But still, living without her will be hard. Although I have no heart, I feel as if I do when it comes to Jewel.

The time Jewel and I have spent together have been some of the best days of my existence.

I will miss her kissing me. Looking at me with her sad eyes, and her damn stubbornness.

I laugh to myself thinking about her.
I swore off women once before, and I can do it again.
My plan is to let her go now, to live her life freely. Then

Donna Tischner

I'll go home to Romania.

Kiss Of Life

Chapter 16:
LIVE AND LET LIVE

I haven't seen Roman in days. I'm not even sure he's here in the USA anymore. I tried to call him on his cell phone, but he never answers.

I'll text him again.

> "Roman? are you okay?
> Please answer me.
> I love you."

I waited for his reply, but he never responded. I decided to tell him once more in a text before ending our relationship how I felt, so I texted him again.

> "I love you so much!
> Please don't do this to me.
> Answer me, please."

Two hours went by, and still no reply from him. All I could do was cry.

Donna Tischner

I lied in bed for a week, crying my heart out over him.

Thinking about everything we've been through; *he's just going to let us go. Is it that easy? Really?*

I got out of bed and showered. Then walked across the street to see if Roman was there. I knocked and knocked, but there was no one home.

Then I decided to fly to Romania. I booked my flight and was in the air by that night.

When I landed at Sibiu International Airport, I hailed a taxi and went to the Castle.

After some time, the guards let me in, and I knocked on the door. Belvidere greeted me gallantly with kisses. Then he asked what I was doing there: I told him I need to see Roman, and I wasn't leaving until I spoke to him.

Belvidere told me he was in the study and he wouldn't have visitors at the moment and that I should wait in the Parlor for him. I told him that was fine. He brought me in a drink as I waited.

Kiss Of Life

As I convened on the sofa, I knew, Roman knew I was already there waiting. I figured he wasn't going to see me. But I waited hours anyway.

When finally, Belvidere told me Roman has gone out on business and wouldn't be back till dawn. I burst out in tears. I sat there staring up at him, questioning why Roman wouldn't see me. But he couldn't tell me anything.

Belvidere brought me to my feet, then wrapped his arms around my back, caressing me. I cried on his shoulder, saying why, over and over. Belvidere then called for their Limo and watched as we drove away. I went to an Athene Palace Hilton Bucharest, A Hotel, overlooking the City.
I stayed in the Presidential Suite and enjoyed the balcony looking out at the scenery. Although I cried a lot, none of the sights mattered. I only thought about Roman.

Two days later, I went down to the bar to have a drink and be around people. I sat at the counter sipping my Zombie, and playing with the straw inside the glass, swirling it around in circles. A gentleman spoke to me, and I didn't hear him until he tapped me on my shoulder. I looked up at him in concern; then, he asked to buy me a drink. When I said, "sure," he spoke saying, "You must have a lot on your mind, I was speaking to you, and you didn't hear me." I smiled, not commenting.

Then he asked my name and if I was staying in the hotel alone. I didn't want to answer him, but I told him, "My name is Jewel; I'm waiting on my friend." I didn't want to talk to him; I had too much on my mind to think about other men. I thanked him for the drink and excused myself.

As I was stepping off my stool, I caught myself falling; my arms grabbed the seats on the side of me. *I only had two drinks,* I thought to myself. How could I be this drunk? I felt myself going down and like the lights were turning off. Was I drugged? I need to fight this. Who is this guy? I stumbled to the doorway, and that man followed me.

I was going down; he caught me under my arms, saying, "I have you." I told him to take his hands off of me, but he started to pick me up. I began calling Roman, telepathically, "help me, I'm in trouble!"
But Roman didn't come...

Again, I told the man to let me go, but he carried me out of the bar. I tried to call for help, but no words were coming out of my mouth. I grabbed the door jamb, but my fingers slipped off as he tugged me through the

Kiss Of Life

doorway. I kicked as much as I could, it felt like I wasn't even moving.

My eyes started closing; I told myself to fight it, stay awake. But my eyes were getting too heavy to keep open.

What was this guy going to do with me? Rape me? Murder me? Both?
"OH God, Roman, please help. I'm about to die."
My eyes shut. I was out cold.

***

Romania's POV

Belvidere told me Jewel is here in Romania, but I already knew that. She's staying in a Luxury Hotel in the next town over.

I felt her pain, her tears. I ached for her. Jewel's is the only thing I think of all day long.

Leaving her in the USA was hard, not saying goodbye. But

it was for her good. I want her to go on with her life.

I want nothing more than to run to her hotel and hold her.

I feel her calling me. She's in trouble. Big trouble. I tell Belvidere, "Jewel's needs me." Belvidere questions, "What do you mean?" "Someone has her." "Well, are you going to help her?" "I can't; she needs to figure this one out on her own."

I walked away from Belvidere, feeling bad. He yells to me as I'm walking, " you have to help her!" His voice was like a knife cutting my throat.

***

"Where am I?" I asked the man. But he didn't respond. I'm in a hotel room; I see the City through the windows. "Mr. what are you doing?"

I try to pick my head up, but it's spinning. My arms feel heavy, like I can't move them. I'm strapped to his bed. "Romanian, please come, help."

"The man has a knife. I see bottles on his table, chloroform? it read. "Shit! what do I do?"

Kiss Of Life

I can't believe Roman didn't come to my rescue.

The man steps closer to me, then says, "This will only hurt for a few seconds. If you scream, I'll make it hurt longer." He aims the sharp blade over my belly, presses the tip of the knife into my flesh.

I scream! I screamed so loud the man jerked back. My blood is running down the side of my rib cage. Then there's banging on the hotel door.

"Are you alright in there?" "Help me please! HELP!" "What's going on in there?" I'm calling the Police!"

The man comes at me again, knife pointing at my face. I try to move my head away, turning my face from him, but he grabs my cheeks.

I said a quick prayer, and then Roman grabbed the man, biting into his throat and ripping out his vocal cords. He untied me. He picked me up in his arms and flew us back to the Castle.

Once Roman had me, I passed out, from the loss of blood. He put me down on the foyer floor, trying to wake me up, but I wasn't waking.

Roman listened for a heartbeat, but it was fading. He then bit into his wrist, causing himself to bleed, putting the blood to my lips to drink.

Roman couldn't get me to open my mouth to drink. He squeezed my cheeks so hard, causing my lips to pucker and open, dripping his blood into my mouth. When finally, my eyes opened. I was looking up at Roman. I smiled.

He grabbed me holding me tight. He began to speak to me, saying, "I thought I lost you! Princess." Smiling bigger, I reached up and grabbed him, crying into the crook of his neck. He held me, rubbing the back of my hair.

He lifted me again in his arms and carried me to his bedroom. Then he lifted my blouse to show me there were no scars or marks from the man's knife. Roman asked what I was doing with him, but I told him I wasn't with him; he drugged me in the bar.

"Thank you Roman, for saving my life." "It's over now, and your safe with me." "What happens now, you and me?" "What do you want to happen?"

"I want to be with you! I want to marry you! Can't you see

Kiss Of Life

that?" "This cannot be, I want you to live your life, have children." "No, I don't want that lifestyle; I want you!"

"You will one day wish you had a child, and I will not be responsible for you not having a baby." "Please, Romanian."

I sat up, placing my hand in his, bringing it to my lips and holding it there, kissing his fingers, and stroking the top of his hand; tears fell on our laps as I kissed his hand with more feelings, "I love you; you know I do!"

"I do. I cannot deny your love for me." "Roman, I know you love me, or you wouldn't care about my life without a baby."

Roman stands, walking to the other side of the room; he looks back at me, he smiles, then says,
"You will have resentment towards me." "Why do I feel like I have to beg you? I'll beg, if that's what you need, do you want proof of my love?" "No, I already know your love is genuine."

"Then what is the problem? I'm not leaving you again; you'll have to throw me out of this Castle!"

Donna Tischner

Roman walks back over to the bed, sits beside me, and then spoke, "You are so damn stubborn!" He grabs me and begins kissing me all over my face, my neck, and whispers in my ear, "I'm glad you came here." I looked at him and began undressing him.
His kisses became passionate.

We spent the next three days in bed, not leaving each other's side. Belvidere brought us in our meals.

Roman and I couldn't be separated, since being back together.

 He possessed me in his sweet desire.
Whispering poems of enchanting passion. His sweet nothings had me in awe.

After I showered and dressed for breakfast, Roman grabbed my arm, pulling me towards him; he kissed me on my cheek and then said, "I enjoyed this time together with you; these last three days have been like nothing I have ever experienced before. We are to be married this weekend because I never want to let you out of my arms again.

Roman arranged the Wedding, preparing the Castle,

Kiss Of Life

inviting all his friends back for the big day.

Tessa and the girls help me. Fixing my hair and makeup, getting my Gown ready, and all the decorations in the Ballroom.

To keep things traditional, Tessa wouldn't let me see Roman for a whole day. Not seeing him was making me very depressed, and they knew it.

While Roman saw to the festivities, the girls kept me busy in my room.

Then Roman asked Belvidere to walk me down the aisle, Belvidere was ecstatic and eager to please. I too was happy he excepted.

When that big day came, my nerves were a mess. *All those people,* I thought to myself.

Then Tessa and the girls told me they had a big surprise for me. Keeping me wondering, they told me to turn around and close my eyes.

Misty, Lena, and Rochelle spun me, telling me to open my eyes now, I open them, and to my amazement, Brooke, Jack, and Kim are standing in front of me. My friends from back home, in the USA. I ran over to them, hugging all three simultaneously, smearing my makeup, and messing up my hair in my excitement.

It was a surprise from Romanian. He wanted them to be here for me and made it happen. Having them stay with us in the Castle for the week.

They were dressed in wedding attire, looking like models from a fashion magazine.

We redid my hair and makeup. Then Belvidere came walking in, saying, "It's time." My heart started racing like wild horses running through the fields. My palms began to sweat, and my nerves were shaking in my skin.

Brook took me by my hand, saying, "You look so beautiful, and this is going to be great." Tessa told me to take a deep breath, and Lena held my hand as we walked over to Belvidere.

Jack, Kim, and Brook walked with us down the many stairs till we were at the bottom, and then they took their seats in the Chapel.

Misty and Tessa did a beautiful job on the decorations.

Kiss Of Life

The flowers blossomed in total capacity, draped over the many pews, and the red carpet was rolled out as we walked down the aisle. Belvidere held my arm so tight as we approached the altar. Seeing Roman made me smile, and I felt tears line my eyes.

Roman stood there in his Black three-piece Tuxedo, looking more dapper than ever.

His ushers took their position next to him. And the bridesmaids attained their stance holding their bouquets.

Belvidere place my hand in Romanian's hand and then kissed me sweetly on my cheek, taking his seat.

I looked up at Roman, and his face glowed with reverence. I smiled back at him, taking a deep breath.

After our vows, Roman kissed my lips, telling me how happy he is. When Roman smiled, and I thought to myself, it isn't often I get to see him so happy. I enjoyed the moment.

Roman and I went into another room before entering the Ballroom for privacy. We entered the Study, champagne and fruit baskets dressed the tables for us. Roman grabbed me, saying, "We did it! We're Married!" Then he picked up my hand, placing kisses up my arm to my shoulder, then my neck, until he kissed my lips, telling me how happy he is and how much he loves me. I smiled at him, kissing Roman back.

When it was time to enter the Ballroom, Joy and cheers filled the room.

After the Celebration, Roman took me to a Castle in Transylvania for our Honeymoon night. He promised me a memorable Honeymoon after our guests leave in a few weeks.

The Castle was gorgeous. Gold drapes grazed the windows, and candelabras sat on knee-length pillars. It took my breath away.

Roman walked me to our Suite, up the majestic sweeping staircase.

Balconies overlooking the banisters and Chandeliers of crystal hung from the glass ceilings.

Once in our Suite, Roman took me in his arms and began kissing me. He gently laid me down on the bed, undressing me.

Kiss Of Life

The night was filled with desire for each other.

Later we sipped Champagne on the terrace. Then Roman said he needed to tell me something significant. I looked up at him with great turmoil on my face. This was going to be bad; I know it!

"I want you to drink from me my blood. We need to prepare for something that is coming. I will need to drink from you as well to see into the future."

Roman sent my heart into great displeasure. I began asking questions.

"You're giving me bad news on my honeymoon night? What is coming? Who is it?"
"Armies. Of 100's, will come for us soon."
"But why?"
"Princess, these are Vampires, in a desperate need to get to you."

"I'm so confused. What about everyone that was at our Wedding tonight? they want me dead too?"

"No. But others do. They somehow found out your blood is rare. Now they want to taste it."

Donna Tischner

"What do you mean my blood is rare?"

After Roman explained to me about my blood, I sat there in great distress. Unbelieving my parents wouldn't tell me.

I winced in my seat and sipped my drink. I felt my blood drain from me hearing all of this, and my head felt like it was going to explode. I knew I had rare blood, but Roman explained it in more detail. Roman came to me, kneeling, placing his hands on my lap. Then said, "I know this is much to take in, and I apologize, but we need to prepare soon."

Kiss Of Life

Chapter 17:
BLOOD WARS

After a week, Roman and I started to prepare for what is coming.

Roman poured us wine as we sipped it, lolling on the sofa in our bedroom.

He pulled me closer to him, placing his arm around my shoulder. Then he kissed me on my cheek.

I moved onto Roman, straddling him.
I touched his face, gently stroking his cheeks. Then I placed a soft kiss on his lips.
He opened his mouth, allowing our tongues to swirl around. He moved his lips to my throat, kissing me and then over my breast. I moaned in delight. He groaned from my excitement.

I felt him growing under my legs. Telling me, he wants me. I moved my hips over him, pulling his shirt out of his pants to gain access to his chest, bringing my lips to the flesh of his sexy Ab's.

Donna Tischner

Roman grabbed me, unzipping my black chiffon dress, sliding it down, I felt his lingering skin brush my chest, possessively he lifted me to the wall, with my legs around his waist.

He dragged his tongue along me, kissing me all over my shoulders, my breasts, and tracing his lips to my mouth.

Holding Roman around his neck biting, sucking, and kissing him there. His pants getting tighter around his groin. He unzipped them, pulling them down and sliding into me. Using the wall to hold us up, he bit into my neck. I can feel my blood dripping down my collarbone.

As he roared, making me want him more, he then carried me to the bed. Biting into his wrist, having me drink his blood. I held Roman's wrist to my lips, in delight, drinking of him. He tried to pull it away after a few seconds, but I craved more. He drew away, saying, "No more. You can't have too much."

"Please, just a little more."

He gave me a look, and then Roman put his wrist back to my mouth and let me taste him a little longer.

Kiss Of Life

He was like drinking black coffee without the sugar. I felt more robust and vigorous with his blood flowing throughout my body. I wanted to scream in wonder.

Roman let out a laugh holding me in his arms. Then he said, "You're going to be an Insubordinate Vampire."

I looked at him with a devious smile telling him to bring his ass back to bed. I need to finish what he started on the sofa. He laughed more and climbed back into the bed with me.

Later during the night, he woke me telling me to drink more of his blood. Reopening the wound on his wrist, I drank. I felt like I could fly. My head spun in wonder, and my body gave off a strong energy.

Roman, I said, what is happening to me?
Roman told me our blood was dancing and needed release of all that energy soon, or I would be zapping everything in sight. He was testing my body out with the amount of blood he had given to me.

He brought me into the gym, in the castle. Weights and punching bags, and all sorts of machinery stood in front of me. Telling me to go crazy, zap everything he said.

Donna Tischner

I zapped the punching bag, and it flew off the chain hanging from the ceiling. Next, I zapped the dumbbells on the floor, they crashed into the mirrors on the wall, shattering. I had the agility of a Vampire and the power to kill anything in my path.

Roman stood back and watched as I tore up the room, releasing much of that force.
I heard him laugh with great pleasure and watched as he shook his head back and forth.

Not long after, I zapped the shit out of the weight room, Roman began to have a vision. He fell to the floor. His eyes became red with heat. His voice was like a demon. He yelled for me to leave the room in fear he would hurt me.

I ran and told Belvidere, and we waited together for Roman to come to us.

After a while, the doorbell sounded. Belvidere and I looked at each other, wondering who it could be at the door in this late hour. We went to answer it; Belvidere opened the door, and a Vampire came at me with the speed of light. I tried to zap him, but he held my hands down and got on top of me. Before I could do anything. It was too late.

Romanian's POV

"Don't open that door! Wait..."
I flew as fast as I could down the stairs. I ripped the Vampire off Jewel.
When I looked at his face, I realized it was Jeremy. I haven't seen him in a year.
I grabbed Jeremy and threw him across the floor, sliding into the wall, cracking the drywall.

He got up with force coming at me. We flipped each other a few times, landing on the marble tiles. The tiles shattered, and splinters shot up in the air. Jeremy came at me again, trying to jump on my back and bite me. I flipped him over my shoulder, pinning him to the floor. Then I picked up the marble splinter stabbing it into Jeremy's heart. He grabbed the fragment, holding it with both hands still embedded in him. Squirming on the bloody tile. Whimpering, he said, "I just wanted to taste her, I wasn't going to hurt Jewel, I heard about her blood." I kick the motherfucker in the face, and he closed his eyes, his body burst into flames and disintegrated into ash.

I saw Jewel on the floor, not breathing. I reached over her

body on the floor. Trying to breathe life back into her lungs. I pressed onto her chest, she sat up like a stiff Vampire in a coffin. Letting out an exasperated breath.

Belvidere called her name. Jewel's turned her head towards him, but she didn't speak a word. I looked at Belvidere, he looked back at me, waiting for Jewel's to talk, but she didn't. I was unsure, was she a Vampire? I didn't know what to expect with her rare blood. Was it possible?

Jewel's acted more like a Zombie. Not moving. Not talking. Just staring off into the distance.
I slid my hands under Jewel's body, lifting her in my arms, then carrying her to our bedroom. Lying her on our bed.

The wind blew the French double doors open in our room. White clouds of moisture swirled around and swiveled in circles, seeking out Jewel's, kissing her on the lips.

She sat up, looking at me, then said, "Roman."
I ran to her bedside, caressing her in my arms, kissing her, and clearing the hair off Jewel's face.
I asked her, "are you okay?" She nodded her head yes. Then she said,

Kiss Of Life

"I was with my mother. She took me to a faraway place. I have never seen anything like it on this planet.
 Blues, purples, reds, and greens like I have never beheld. Flowers like symphonies. And animals of love.
I saw oceans so clear and sand-like gold.

Then my mother told me something about herself.

A Vampire for seen her in a schoolyard, he stalked her, then kissed her on her mouth. My mother asked him not to stop kissing her. He then placed his mouth to her collarbone and bit into her neck, drinking of her.

 He asked her to swallow his blood, and he would find her whenever she needed him. His blood laid dormant.

This Vampire was Jeremy. His and my parent's blood caused my rare blood. Giving me these powers. Jeremy Found out my mother conceived and wanted to meet the girl that could have been his daughter.

But then my mother told me not to trust him; he would smell me and wouldn't be able to stop drinking of me.
They were in love and wanted to be together. But she was already married.

From time to time, Jeremy would visit her; he would take

her to places worldwide and have her back that same night.

I asked her why she is telling me all of this. She said I needed to know I was different, unlike anyone in this world.

And soon, I would learn how to control my powers without the blood of a Vampire.

***

"Roman, I need to learn more about these powers. I need you to help me."

Belvidere stood by my bed and offered some help. He told me he could take me to a man that might know something about them. But Roman insisted it was not safe, and the man should come to us. Belvidere would arrange for him to meet with me.

A few days later the man came to our Castle. He wouldn't tell us his real name and told us we should call him Magic.

Kiss Of Life

Magic was an odd man, short and heavy. Balding and talked with a lisp. The hair he had, was white and his mustache curled up over his lips.

He blew his nose often and then coughed afterwards. I found him to be quite peculiar but funny.

We stepped into the Parlor, and he examined me with an elope Gold Monocle Steampunk, between his fingers.
I thought it was kind a weird that he used that.

Walking around me in circles until he said,
"You have an energy that flows with color." "What does that mean?" I asked.
He said rather forwardly, "Your color is singing and dancing within you; it needs to be released."

Again, I asked, "What does that mean?"

"It means those powers need a release, or you will burst, at the peak of them.

It means your body can contain only so much energy; when it's nearly complete, the power reverses, and the consequences can be devastating.

To release it, you must do as Romanian had you doing.

Zap everything. Until it's gone."

Your color is bright within you, which means you have a heart of gold. I can feel its aura all around you. It's pretty powerful. But if someone crosses you, I'd hate to be the one in your way. You'll split them into pieces."

We all just stood there in amazement, thinking about what Mr. Magic said.

I asked him, "am I a walking time bomb?" He laughed and said, "You could be." In all seriousness. Then he said, "You have the power to control them; only you can figure out how to do that."

Roman showed him to the door. And we remained in the Parlor for some time. Finally, heading up the stairs to go to sleep.

In the middle of the night, Roman woke with another vision. I watched as he stepped off the bed and grabbed his head and keeled over to the floor. He picked his head up and said, "they're on their way; get ready!"

I changed my clothes, putting on black spandex and a black form-fitting longs sleeve shirt to move quickly.

Kiss Of Life

Belvidere stayed in his room and locked his doors, keeping still and quiet.

We waited until they burst down the Rod Iron fence and made their way to the front doors.

Roman gave me more of his blood, and I was so wind up and ready.

They banged on the doors and hit them again, yelling too, "give her to us!"

Roman became angry, and the doors were kicked down.

Hundreds of Vampires came pooling in the Castle, storming us. I zapped a hundred of them, slicing them in half, and Roman created a wind force that sent another hundred back into the walls. But when they saw the Vampires split in half, the others backed off. But I wasn't finished. I zapped another fifty of them, slicing limbs off their bodies; they pleaded for their lives. But Roman wasn't done either with them. In his Rage, he became a Demon, showing them who he really is.

When his skin turned grey and his veins bulged out of his body, the Vampires tried to flee the Castle. But he grabbed one, biting his throat and ripping his tongue out of him from his neck.

 The blood war went on until every one of them was dead. I checked the grounds outside for stragglers but didn't see any. Roman checked on Belvidere, making sure he was okay.
Then we stood there looking at all the dead bodies and the bloody mess that spilled on our foyer floor. Belvidere told us to go upstairs and get some rest, and he would take care of the mess.

Roman and I proceeded up and showered.

Roman took me in his arms, holding me there, then he said, "I am so proud of you! you handled that very well." He kissed me, and we fell asleep.

Chapter 18:
BELVIDERE

Now that this Blood War is over, Romanian and Jewel can have their proper honeymoon. They deserve it after the last couple of months. They came through everything with shining colors.

I need a drink... Walking over to the bar, I pour myself a stiff glass of Whiskey.

Cleaning this Castle of all its blood has taken a toll on me, after all these years, I'm feeling tired now. Romanian will never let me retire, and I feel as if my body needs a break now.
 I have no home to speak of and no family to welcome me back. I've been with Romanian for so long I never had the chance to have a family of my own. I was giving him my all since we first met.

Sipping my Whiskey and walking over to the desk to sit. I take out the pen and paper.

I missed out on having a wife and children, but I always loved Romanian like a son. He was just a boy when I met

Donna Tischner

him. A boy stuck in an immortal body...

My heart was always heavy for what happened to him in the woods that evening. When that creature took his life. I saw something in his eyes. His pain would endure for the rest of his life being immortal. And it would hurt me too. He told me the story, and my heart shattered. He was too young.

The day he told me he is immortal, I couldn't understand what he was saying, I was trying hard to make it register, Romanian had to show me his fangs, to make me understand. He told me he needs blood to survive, and I still could not comprehend. The shock of his story tore me up.

Putting my hand to my forehead, shaking my head back and forth as I remember him telling me, with blood tears in his eyes.

I've always thought of him as fair, honest, and loyal.
He has always been there for me and never let me down. All my days with Romanian, he's treated me very well. I don't think I've ever told him that.

I must make a note of it to tell him.

Kiss Of Life

I've seen him bring other women into his Castle, but he never fell in love with them. He was never going to let love back into his life, especially after his wife, Justina. No matter how many times I told him, love would come to you one day, and there's not going to be anything you can do about it. He believed it was not possible to love again, not fair to love a woman, and he would never let that happen.

I have seen a lot of ladies falling over him, but he called them whores.

Woman came and went. They never spoke back to him or ridiculed him. Not that he would allow that. I've seen a few of these ladies try to steal from him. They paid the price. I've seen them try to make him fall in love with them, but he was never interested in romance or love. Sex was all he used them for. Not even their blood did he want.

I wasn't too keen on those ladies either. They never seemed natural or suitable for him.

It had been decades since I saw Romanian with a woman he cared about when Jewel came into his life. I knew she was the one for him.

Donna Tischner

I thought at; first, it was her blood he wanted, and it was, but I also knew that he would never let a woman talk to him the way she did.

A few times, I thought he would kill her, just drain her of all her blood. But he didn't. She's made him mad at times, yes; I have seen him throw fits of rage and cause the house to shake, I've seen objects dart across the rooms, and I've seen him strangling her. Jewel was the only one that made him mad like that. Jewel's is one tough girl. She stuck it out through thick and thin. Winning his heart. But she wasn't trying to win his heart, I don't even think she liked him in the beginning.

Seeing him happy now makes me feel like he can finally go on with his life. Being wanted and cared for by someone who loves him as much as he loves her.

Standing, I grab some more Whiskey and stare out the window. The sky is clear, and the weather is getting warmer now. Better days are coming.

Wherever they decide to live, whether here in Romania or the USA, I know they'll be happy. That's all I care about now.

Kiss Of Life

Too many times, I have seen him depressed and sitting alone. Many nights, I sat with Romanian while he talked about taking his own life for what he had become. The hurt I felt for him, the pain we would share together, quietly, as he would never have children.

He spoke of kids many times. And how he would have been a good father. He was smiling about it.

He shared with me his secret about Jewel's never having children if she married him; I told him that was her decision. And there are still ways she can have a baby with you. Romanian just smiled at me. Then he thanked me for being a friend to him. But in all honesty, he is my son—the one I never had.

When he came to me and asked me to walk Jewel down the aisle, I was enamored by him. He touched my heart in a way nothing ever has.
Jewel's too; she gave me a gift, not just the bracelet, but the gift of having the opportunity to walk my daughter down the aisle and give her away to the man who has been nothing but great to me. To me, she is beautiful, intelligent, witty, and loving. Her beauty will endure forever, and all others will want to be close to her.

Donna Tischner

I will miss him dearly. I will miss Jewel's too.
My time here is almost done now. My age has caught up to me. Life without Romanian will be difficult. It's the only life I ever knew. But I need to rest now.
I feel my eyes tearing up. I don't believe I have ever cried before. But the thought of leaving pains me so.

I turned from the window and wiped my eyes with my fingers. Tears dripped off my hand and down to the floor. I cannot believe I'm this upset.

Romanian and I have been through so much together.
There will be no goodbyes. I know Romanian will try to make me stay if I tell him goodbye. He needs to live his life with his wife now and let me go. I will leave a note explaining this all to him. He will have no choice but to accept it.
 My job is done here. And I can retire. I can sleep.

Kiss Of Life

Chapter 19:
ROMANIAN & JEWEL

It's been over a month since our ordeal on the blood wars. Roman and I have finally set a date to have our memorable Honeymoon on the Cayman Island. We will be staying in a Castle overlooking the crystal turquoise water.

Our flight leaves in two days, and we have been busy packing for a three week stay.

I need Belvidere's help, so I'm walking to his room to ask him.
I knocked on his door, but he didn't reply. I'm guessing he's downstairs fixing breakfast.

Roman sees me in the hallway, stopping me for a kiss. I smile, saying, "Good morning my husband." He answers me back, with kisses to my lips. I smile taking his hand continuing down the corridor.

Then Roman asks me what I'm doing when I explain I'm

looking for Belvidere. Roman walks with me down to the dining room in search of Belvidere. But he's not around.

We call for him, but he doesn't answer. We walk searching the Castle, going from room to room. Roman walks into the foyer, he sees a note on the big round table, picking it up and reading it. When Roman says, "He's gone." I look up at him, asking, "what do you mean?" Roman is holding a note in his hand and then tells me, "this is from Belvidere." I run to his side and begin to read the letter with Roman.

My eyes tear up right away, and Roman puts the note down on the table, walking out of the room. I lift the letter holding it in between my fingers, staring at it in shock. I run after Roman. Calling to him to stop, wait, but he keeps walking.

I reach him and grab his arm, asking Roman if he's OK, but he tells me, "No, I'm not OK; that man is like a father to me. He just upped and walked out of my life; how could he do that? He's been with me for almost 65 years. I treated him well! I gave him everything!"
"Roman, the letter said he was tired and needed to rest now, he knew goodbyes wouldn't be easy, that's why he did it this way."

Kiss Of Life

"I'm going to look for him and bring him back here!"
"He doesn't want to work anymore; he's getting too old. bring him back to live out his days here, not to work."
Roman's hand grazes my cheek, and he smiles at me. Then he kisses my lips telling me he'll be back soon.
After some time, I headed back to my room; I couldn't even pack because I was too upset. All I could think about was, *I hope Roman finds him and brings him home to us.*

Romanian's POV:

I glided the sky and skimmed the trees to all the places I thought Belvidere would go, when I found him in a bar sitting at a table alone, sipping his drink, in deep thought. I saw a tear hit the table and I called to him.

"Belvidere?" I asked if I could sit when he nodded his head, looking down at his Whiskey.

Then I asked him, "Are you alright? I too was upset, but I needed to hear him out.
He said with a heavy voice, "Romanian, I'm sorry. I couldn't say goodbye to you."

Donna Tischner

I stopped him mid-sentence, putting my hand up to quiet him some, "It's OK, I understand. We want you to come home."

Belvidere picked his head up, staring at me. More tears fell from his eyes, and then he said, "I'm old now and tired, you gave me a full life with everything I needed, but I can no longer do this."

"I understand, and I don't want you to work for us now; I want you to come home and be a father to me."
Belvidere continued to watch me; my expressions said it all. I reached across the table taking Belvidere's hands in mine.

"Really? be your father?"
A coy smile formed at his mouth; he was so cute, as he sat there staring at me. Then he pulled his hands back as he played with his drink, swirling the whiskey around in his glass.

A few minutes went by and no words were spoken. He put his drink down on the table and then, Belvidere stood and walked over to me putting his arms out to hold me.
I stood up and grabbed him, holding him, and telling him,

Kiss Of Life

"don't ever leave me again! you're my family; you always have been."

He then said to me,
"All those years I listened to you about not having a family,"
I watched as his shoulders became heavy, and he heaved deep breaths, crying; he put his head down and then continued to say,
" When I was leaving, I realized I had no one, no place to go, no family of my own; you were all I ever had, I knew no other life."

I felt like shit when he said that. I never even asked him what he thought about marriage. For himself. I apologized to him for being so selfish. But he stopped me, saying, "I could have told you, but I never thought about it."

I put my arm around his shoulder, and we left the bar.
Once they were back in the Castle, I ran to Belvidere and held him, taking his luggage from his hands, and bringing it to his room.
Then Roman told him, "we need to get another butler." Belvidere said, it is already done, and he should be here shortly.
Not long after the doorbell sounded, Roman went to the

door, and a gentleman stood before him saying he is, Alfred Bennet, your new butler.

Roman showed him in, and they went over the house rules and other details.

Alfred stood about 6 feet 2 inches; he was tall, thin, and good-looking. He was mid 40's with salt and pepper hair. Alfred wore a Tuxedo with tails and white gloves. I thought he was polite and charming.

Roman and I watched him as the day went on, and Belvidere thought he would work out simply fine.

We dressed for dinner, having Belvidere join us, and Alfred came in holding an envelope and saying to Roman, "Excuse me, Sir, but this just came for you."

Roman took the letter and began to read it. When he looked up at me, saying, "It seems we will have a visitor for the next two days, they'll be here this evening." I asked, "Who?" "Brook and Angel Winters." My mouth dropped to the floor. Surprised by this, I asked Roman if they said why? He told me, "Brook's mother is Romanian and was coming to see her relatives here in Romania."

Kiss Of Life

We sat in the parlor after dinner for drinks when our guests arrived. Alfred showed them in, and I jumped up, grabbing Brook, then greeting her mother. After the introductions, Alfred showed them to their rooms.

It has been a year since I saw Angel, she is attractive with her long gray hair, she wore in an updo very stylish. Angel still had a magnificent figure, and her blue dress was very becoming of her. Even though she was in her late 60's, she was exceptionally beautiful.

Belvidere asked Angel if she would like a drink, and he poured her a glass of wine handing it to her. They seemed to hit it off very well. Brook and I sat around and talked for hours. Roman went into his office to finish his work.

Later, Brook said she was tired and needed to sleep from their long flight. I went into Roman's office; the lights were dim and the mood somber. Roman told me to come over to him, waving his hand for me to sit on his lap. When I sat, my back to his chest, he pulled the hair off my neck and kissed me there. I moaned from his touch. He wrapped his arms around my stomach, holding me; he said, "You are so beautiful." I turned and smiled, kissing him. Then there was a knock at the office door. It was Belvidere. I stood up, and he entered the room, saying, "I hope I'm not interrupting; I just came in here to thank you

Roman stood, walking over to him, telling Belvidere, "there is nothing to thank us for; this is your home too." I couldn't help but say, "Belvidere, ever since I met you, you have been the kindest man to me.

 I want you to know, you are like a father to me, and I love you."

I saw tears lining his eyes; then he wiped them with his fingers saying, "I am so happy for you, Romanian, you have found a beautiful wife, and I see how happy you are." Wiping more tears from his eyes and cupping Roman's shoulder, he continued to say, "All these years we have been together, I always wanted to see you happy, with the one woman who would truly love you, for who you are, and I see now you have found her."

I felt the sting in my eyes; I couldn't help but feel so touched by his words. Roman held Belvidere telling him, "Thank you." Then Roman said,
"Now we need to find you a companion." Belvidere let out a laugh shaking his head back and forth, saying, "no, I am too old."

Kiss Of Life

We left the office together, heading up the stairs to bed; when Angel said she was lost and couldn't remember where her bedroom was, Belvidere said he would show Angel to her room.

In the morning, we all met for breakfast as we watched Alfred getting used to his new surrounding and being so attentive to us. I asked Alfred how he slept and if he had all the accommodations he needed.

He thanked me, saying, yes, he slept well, and everything in his room was to his satisfaction.

The weekend passed, and we said our goodbyes to Brook and Angel as we were setting off for our Honeymoon. They asked if they could stop back after they visit with the family.

Roman and I sat in the Jet as we made our way to the Cayman Islands.
We have been looking forward to this for some time.

After we arrived, and the Limousine brought us to the Castle, Roman grabbed me, carrying me over the threshold; I laughed as he kissed me then put me down in the foyer. We both stood there looking around; it was so beautiful.

The staircase is lined in 24 carat gold, with white marble tiles. Columns grazed the long corridor with sconce lighting. The colors were greys and black on the walls as we approached our bedroom.

The four-poster bed with a black canopy draped down the sides on the bedframe. It was simply gorgeous.

We neared the bed, and I let myself fall back onto the mattress with my arms spread out like I was flying.

Roman came over to me on the bed and pulled me onto his lap; I leaned up and kissed him on his forehead, pulling his hair back and stroking his chest. He moaned in his delight and flipped us; he was on top of me. He pulled my blouse over my head and kissed my breasts over my bra.

I couldn't help but cry out for him to keep going. He smiled devilishly and unbuttoned his trousers, kissing his way to my thighs. I helped Roman out of his shirt, unbuttoning it and pulling it over his shoulders. I kissed him there as his hands worked their way to my breasts. I moaned again, loving his gentle touch, and he pulled himself on top of me, moving his hips on mine and

Kiss Of Life

caressing my back. He licked my neck, his soft tongue, wet and cold, when he bit into me, loving, and savoring the extraction. I heard him growl in his moment of pleasure. Roman grabbed my hand, making our fingers entwine; he held them over my head squeezing my fingers in his passion. His cold skin rubbed against mine; he said to me how he loved when my flesh warmed him, that it made his bones feel alive.

We laid in bed till the morning with Roman's arms wrapped around me, letting me feel so secure.

In the morning, he joined me in the shower, the warm water trickled over our heads, running down our face, and he grabbed me, pinning me to the cold tile wall. My legs wrapped around his waist and my arms stroking his hair. He kissed me all over my face, then he snuck his tongue into my mouth, letting me know how aroused he is. I laughed as I kissed him back.

We spent the day shopping and eating. And We spent the night on the beach around a campfire.
We took long romantic walks along the shoreline, holding hands and kicking up the water with our feet. Roman squeezed my hand in his, pulling me close to his side and wrapping his arm around my back.

Donna Tischner

After our three-week Honeymoon, it was time to go home. Although we both wanted to stay, we knew we had to get back to the Castle.

Once back in Romania, Alfred greeted us, taking our bags. Belvidere was with Angel holding her hand. And Brook was with Trevor, who unexpectedly stopped over before we left.

Roman and I were pleasantly surprised by the couples that had joined together in our absence.

We made our way upstairs to our bedroom; neither one of us questioned what was going on when Alfred offered some information saying. "We had quite an interesting couple of weeks here, Sir." "What do you mean?" "I learned a lot about who you are and the history of this Castle. Brook had an accident when Trevor brought her back to life, pushing air into her lungs through CPR. Angel was screaming when Belvidere took her in his arms and hadn't let go of her since then.

Roman and I looked at each other in horror; I grabbed my mouth with my hand, gasping in total panic. Asking what the hell happen, Alfred told us,

Kiss Of Life

"Brook fell down the stairs and stopped breathing. When Trevor ran to her aid, she is totally fine now. I watched as his fangs descended and fell back into the wall. Belvidere assured me he would not hurt me. He had to sit me down and explain it to me. I know who you are, Sir, and I will never speak of this to another. You have my word."

I was so confused I had to ask, "Is she...?" Alfred told me, "No, she is still mortal." I let out an exasperated breath, shaking my head. Roman told Alfred he would not want to see him angry, and his word better be solid.

Then Alfred told us that Belvidere and Angel had been together since the incident, and I think he will propose to her soon.

Smiling, Roman and I thanked Alfred for the information and went back downstairs to be with our guests.

Trevor came to me asking if I would mind if he courted Brook. I smiled at him cupping my hand on his shoulder, and then asked him to take good care of her. Giving them our blessing Roman and I sat on the veranda sipping wine and enjoying our time home with everyone.

The wind blew warm air through my hair, and I smiled, feeling the sentiment. The stars were twinkling in the evening sky. Roman told me how happy he is and how much he loves me, thanking me for marrying him. I let out a laugh, stroking his face, telling Roman how much I love and adore him, and thanked him for asking me to marry him. He held me in his arms, standing on the veranda, looking over at the green pastures.

Roman's phone rang, and he looked at it, saying, "I better take this, it seems important." He walked away and then my phone rang, I answered it thinking, this was strange how both our phones rang at almost the same time.

I answered my phone, and it was Sargent Butler telling me he has information about my father's passing, and I need to see you as soon as possible. Roman came to me saying, "We need to head to the States at once."
I tipped my head to him saying, "I just got a phone call from Sargent Butler, we should leave right away. I have a bad feeling about this Roman."

Chapter 20:
BREATHE

We set off for the States making our way to the Jet. An entourage of friends accompanied us.
We sat comfortably for the long flight while we discussed our plans for what's to come.

Roman told me before we left that the phone call he received was from John Tayler, one of his closest friends from way back when.

John had mentioned that the police have been probing around the Victorian house and the wooded area. They found 2 other bodies with marks on their necks.

John keeps watch on the detectives investigating the crime scene. He calls Romanian with updates letting him know the cops found trails of blood leading to the Victorian.

Roman tells me, "Once we're back in NY, you're to go straight to your home and wait for me there. Say nothing about our marriage to anyone." I nod my head in understanding to him.

The Jet lands and we get into a waiting car heading back to my home.

Roman kisses me goodbye telling me he'll see me soon. Brook and Belvidere come with me.

Trevor watches from the trees near the wooded area as Roman pulls into the driveway with his attendants. They exit the vehicle and proceed to the entrance when a police officer stops him for questioning. Romanian's eyes turn red with fire, as he begins to hypnotize the officer, telling him, "you will tell the detectives everything is clear here. There will be no more questions, you will not come to my door again. Don't look back, just go!"

The officer leaves telling the detective the Victorian house checked out ok. Still the police officers stand in the street staring at the house, until another officer calls out, "I found something!" They run to the area, Forensics photograph the scene and bag the evidence. Trevor's eyesight picks up what it was they were bagging and reports back to Romanian. Trevor tells Romanian that the police found a girls bracelet and they have it now for evidence.

Kiss Of Life

Forensics dig through the leaves, finding nothing in the wooded area. Taping off the crime scene a police officer stands guard for the night keeping everyone away from the site.

Romanian walks to the officer asking him what's going on, when the cop tells him they found two more bodies here, Romanian asks, "What happened to them?" The police officer tells him he cannot give any information about an active crime scene. But Romanian hypnotizes him making the officer give him all the information he has. The officer tells him, "Two more bodies have turned up here, they appear to have been stabbed in the chest with a jagged knife, we have a lead on the perpetrator. We're in pursuit now to his house." Romanian asks the officer, "I was told they had bite marks on their necks. Is that not true?" The officer tells Romanian, "There were no bite marks to their necks, they were stabbed." Romanian thanks the policeman and walks away calling John on his phone to come to the Victorian now.

Romanian takes John by the throat holding him against the wall screaming in his face, "You made me come out here, the information you gave me was incorrect! They were murdered not bitten!"

Donna Tischner

He releases John from his grip and John tells him, "I fixed it to look like that! There is a murderer around here, and I set it up to have him captured." Romanian asks who the murder is, and John tells him, "A man called Singer. He lives down the road from here, I've been watching him." But Romanian is still not satisfied, asking, "What does this have to do with Jewel's?" When John tells him, "This Singer guy, has photos of her all over his walls, she was next on his list." Romanian asks him, where is Singer now?" John says, "No one knows."
Romanian speeds to Jewel's house, Trevor behind him and they begin to hear some commotion inside.

Jewel's POV

Once we entered my house, I pulled out a bottle of wine from the bar and we sat drinking near the fireplace.
I heard a thump in my bedroom and got up to check it out.

Kiss Of Life

Belvidere asked me not to go in there alone, but I needed him to sit with Brook and her mom to play it safe. I walked down the hall listening carefully to all the bangs and thumps as I approached my room.

 Feeling a little uneasy about opening my bedroom door, I turned away walking back to the living room.

Belvidere and Alfred asked me, "What is it?" I put my fingers to my lips tell them all to hush for a minute. I waved my hand to them all to follow me out of the house, but just as I was opening the front door, a man came charging me with a knife in his hand. I felt my head tingle and my body heat up like fire, throwing my hand up in the air and zapping the man, his hand went flying across the room with the knife still in it. Brook and Angel gasped in shock as the man's hand detached from his arm. But the man still came at me, blood pouring from his injured arm. Roman came in just as the man charged me again, Roman caught him by the back of his neck, seeing his injuries Roman glided him to his house where the many detectives and police officers were, Roman drops him on the front lawn and glides out of there never being seen.

The policemen see Mr. Singer on the lawn with his hand missing and blood seeping out of his arm asking, "What happen?" Mr. Singer is unable to tell them fearing they wouldn't believe his story.

Once Roman came back to my house, he grabbed me asking if I was alright. I assured him I was fine. The problem wasn't me; it was Brook and Angel.

They wanted to know how I was able to do that. I couldn't give them an explanation, so I just said it was a freak thing. Even Alfred was a bit shocked.

Angel told us she knew Mr. Singer, and he lived near her. They were neighbors. She said, "I always thought he was a little strange. Angel said she had felt sad for him and that she wished she could have helped him. But we had to tell her,

"sometimes you can't fix people. Sometimes, they don't want to be helped. Sometimes, they can't be saved."

The sentiment was nice, but you can't justify for murder.

Later as we all went back to the Victorian, Alfred fixed us dinner and we ate together in the dining room. Angel was still upset over Mr. Singer and said, she wanted to see him. Brook got upset telling her mother, "there is no way

Kiss Of Life

you're going to see him. It's not going to happen!" Belvidere held Angel saying he agreed with Brook and he was sorry her friend turned out like that.

Later that night my cell phone rings and it's Mr. Butler, asking me to come see him in the morning. Agreeing, we hang up.

Roman and I go up to his room calling it a night. It's been another long stressful day, and now all I want to do is sleep.

I close my eyes. Roman pulls me close to him holding me.

In the morning we meet the others for breakfast. Alfred serves us asking if everything is satisfactory. Smiling at him, saying, "Yes."

Not long after we eat, Belvidere is taking me to see Mr. Sargent Butler at the station.
As I enter the precinct, the other officers greet me with smiles and hugs. Belvidere and I walk into Mr. Butlers office. He tells us to sit down. I introduce the two, and then Mr. Butler begins telling me.

"We caught your father's killer." I look at him with a shy smile asking, "who Is he?" He tells me a man named

Singer. He's responsible for many of the deaths in our town. I can't even respond to him, knowing the truth about the other reasons.

I tell Mr. Butler, "thank you for calling me in to tell me this news, I can finally have some closure." Sargent Butler tells me the man will be spending life in prison with no

chance of parole.

Belvidere pats me on my back asking if I'm ready to go, I smile at him saying yes. We stand, shaking Mr. Butlers hand.

Leaving the precinct going back to the Victorian.

When Belvidere opens the door at the Victorian, Roman is standing there waiting to hear what happen. We told him they caught my father's killer, and we can all rest now.

Roman looks at me, smiles, then holds me saying, "I'm sorry about your father, I know how hard this past year has been on you, I hope we can put this all behind us and move forward now."

Kiss Of Life

I smile, holding Roman's hand asking if we can go home now."

Roman asks me, "Romania?" "Yes." He wraps his arms around me saying, "I never thought I would hear you say that."

I said to Roman, "We can Breathe now, maybe now, we can start our lives together, without any more problems."

Roman and I smile as we walk into the parlor, and then Roman's phone rings.

He looks at it, and says, "Now what..."

"Looks like we're going home now to Romania. Somethings going on and we need to get back there at once."

I ask Roman with a nervous voice, "What is it?"
Replying he says, "I have been working on putting together a council for us, and now there's a problem with one of the immortals I chose."

Boarding the Jet, we make our way back to Romania. Being the 12th largest country in Europe, Romania, is located on the southeastern country, of Europe. And it's national capital is Bucharest.

I guess I learned a lot being here, it's such a beautiful country.

I also learned Romania is connected to Russia, having an Embassy in London too.
Romania is noted for their Forests region of Transylvania, ringed by the Carpathian Mountains.

There's so much history here.

After a few hours of flying, Brook came to me asking if she could speak with me in private. I asked her if everything was alright, and she said, "It's Trevor." I looked at her with weary eyes, saying, "What about him?" "I'm in love with him!" I asked her, "Then what's the problem?"
She replied, "There's something different about him, and I'm not sure what it is, I just can't put my finger on it."
I smiled at her saying, "You should ask him, if he loves you, he'll tell you." She smiled back at me and said, "You're right, I'll talk to him now."

Brook set off to talk to Trevor, and I wondered how this was going to turn out here on the Jet. It's better for her

Kiss Of Life

to hear it from him, not me...

Finally, we're descending, and going home to the Castle. Roman comes to me escorting me down the many steps to our car. Like always, he holds me tight next to him on the back seat.

Once we arrived, everyone just wants to settle in and relax, but that's not going to happen any time soon.

Roman takes my hand in his, as we step out of the car. All his servants are standing in a line to greet him, bowing, and grabbing the bags.

We enter the Castle and convene in the Parlor. I walked to the bar and poured myself a drink. Roman came in next asking for a drink too.

Then, we saw him. It was a man I had never met before. Tall, Muscular, with his long blond curls falling over his face. I held his gaze, standing there with the glass leaning on my lips, I froze, and Roman stood in front of me asking him, "Who the hell are you?"

He threw his hands up. Saying, "I'm not here to hurt anyone, I'm a friend, Brooks friend."

Donna Tischner

I swallowed my wine, then placed my hand on Roman's back shoulder, I was nervous, for Brook.

I asked him, "Do you know Brook Waters?"
"Yes." He replied.
"well, what do you want with her?"
"We were engaged, and she upped and left me to come here, I need to know why."

I felt my eyes open wide.
Roman said to him,
"What do we call you?"
"Ralph. Ralph Smith."
"Well Ralph, we'll send for her."

Roman and I leave the parlor and go to our bedroom. Brook passes us on the stairs asking what's going on, I told her, "your ex is downstairs."
She freezes on the steps. Roman and I ask her if she wants to see him, but she turns and runs back to her room.

We meet Brook in her room asking what's going on. She tells us, "Ralph, we we're engaged, to be married, but then my mother needed me to take her here to see her dying aunt. I never told him I was leaving. I just left. A few days later I called him and told him, but then I met Trevor, and now I don't want to be with Ralph."

Brook continued to tell us, "Ralph is much older than me, he's gorgeous and built, but I'm in love with Trevor. I can't believe he flew here to Romania."

Roman tells Brook, "You have to tell him, you owe it to him. Just be truthful."

She looks at us with her big sad eyes, Brook puts her head down, and begins to cry. Trevor hears her and approaches us, asking, "what's wrong?" when Brook tells him, Trevor asks her if she wants him to talk to Ralph, but she tells him, "I'll do it. I just feel bad."

Brook meets Ralph in the Parlor, she stands in the doorway, he runs to her side, but Brook pushes him away. He asks her, "What is it? What's wrong?" Brook tells Ralph, she met someone and they're happy together, she apologizes to Ralph, but Ralph gets mad and comes at her yelling,

"How could you do this to me? I thought you loved me!"
"I did, I'm sorry."
Ralph asks,
"Who is he? I'll kill him!"
"His name is Trevor, and I wouldn't mess with him."

Donna Tischner

Ralph grabs Brook by her arms, squeezing them and pushing her. She cries out to him, "STOP!"

Trevor rushes down to the Parlor, grabs Ralph and flings him across the room. Ralph stands and brushes himself off, ready to fight Trevor, but Trevor smiles at him, asking Brook if she's ok. Brook holds Trevor's arm, saying she's fine, but Ralph is deeply hurt when Tessa walks into the room.

Tessa tells everyone to calm down, she approaches Ralph taking him by the hand and leading him out of the room. They walk out, onto the veranda, and she explains how sorry she is for his pain. Ralph asks Tessa to take him away from this Castle and she does.

Trevor carried Brook to their room closing the door for privacy.

The next morning, we meet for breakfast as Alfred brings in our meal. The talk around the table is of last nights episode.

Trevor told Brook his secret. And Brook said even though she was nervous about him, she still loves him, and it

Kiss Of Life

didn't madder.

Belvidere never told Angel their family secret.

Sometime later, as everyone convenes in the Parlor, sitting around drinking, Trevor and Brook making out like school kids and Roman in his office working, there's a knock at the door.

Alfred open the door and Ralph come storming in to see Brook, he raises his hands holding a blade, and swings it at everyone.

I ran to block Brook, but he swung it slicing me in my chest.

I hit the floor on my knees, holding my breasts and looking up at him.

Everyone screamed, and Roman ran out of his office.
I felt my body fall more to the floor on my stomach.

Roman grabbed me.
He turned me over on his knees and rubbed my face, his eyes turned red with blood. As his tears fell on us. I couldn't keep my eyes open any longer. Life was leaving my body.

Donna Tischner

Romanian's POV

I held her limp body in my arms and kissed Jewel on her cheeks, then her forehead and then her lips.

Trevor grabbed Ralph and ripped him apart. His body lied there on the floor in his own blood. Brook screamed running over to Jewel, she knelt down beside us, with her hands covering her mouth and her eyes streaming tears. She wept kneeling over, her face to the floor.

But I couldn't concentrate on Brook I needed to focus on my Princess.

I slid my arms under her dying body and flew her up to our room, placing her on the bed.

Her blood all over the blankets and pillows. I told her how much I love her, but there was no response.

Then I whispered to Jewel's,

"My Princess, This is The Kiss Of Life."

Kiss Of Life

I opened my wrist and my blood pooled out, placing it to her lips, I bit into every part of her body hoping my venom will stimulate her to wake up.

She didn't respond.

Jewels long brown hair wrapped around her neck and I pulled it back, wet, and bloody, moving it over her head.

I rubbed her hair, stroking it like a comb as it spilled over the pillow. I couldn't help but weep myself.
As I lied beside her crying over her deceased body.

"Princess, Printesa mea, I love you, come back to me.

My kiss may not have been enough to bring her back.

Downstairs everyone is crying, there is no control here, I need to get everyone together. But I'm not too good myself.

I stand from Jewel's bedside, brush myself off, stare at her for a moment, then turn and leave the room.

Once downstairs I asked everyone to pull it together. I

Donna Tischner

knew how harsh that sounded, but I was angry, I was so mad I wanted to kill someone.

Belvidere came to my side, placing his hand on my arm. Apologizing, but I didn't want to hear it. I told them not to apologize at all.

Then I told them to fix up the chapel for a funeral, Brook let out a mournful cry, I looked at her, holding her gaze.

I needed an alter ready, and lots of flowers. I told them to drape a white silk sheet off the alter for Jewels body to lay on. Then I said call in a priest.

Belvidere and I cleaned Jewel's precious body putting her in a Princess white satin gown. Her hair was washed of all that blood and curled sweetly around her shoulders.

I swept my arms under her body and fell on Jewel crying. My knees hit the floor, with my arms still attached to Jewel. I cried and stayed like that for hours.

Belvidere, began to cry too, he tried to pick me up, but I wouldn't let him. I thought to myself,
"God, this man is so strong minded! No wonder I love him so much!"

Kiss Of Life

I couldn't bear to say goodbye to Jewel's. My heart ached like never before.

Every time I stood to lift her; I fell again. I was becoming like a zombie. I couldn't speak. I couldn't eat. I couldn't drink.

How was I ever going to go on living without her?
I thought about taking my own life, whatever life I had, that was...

For two days, I sat with Jewel's in our bedroom. She was really gone, and I knew It was time to deal with the reality. I also knew this wasn't going to be easy.

I took my shower and dressed for my wife's funeral.

I swept my arms under her body and lifter Jewel in my arms in the air. I bent over and kissed her on the mouth.

Walking down the hall to the many stairs and into the Chapel.

I then placed Jewel's sweet body down onto the Alter, her fingers entwined over her stomach. She laid on the Alter alone in the Chapel.

Donna Tischner

The Priest came walking through the Castle and asked to see Jewel. Alfred showed him the way to the Chapel.

I sat in the Parlor, on a club chair with a small round table to the side of me that held a dim low lamp. My legs crossed and my fingers entwined. Not speaking. I didn't want to see anyone. I liked being a lone for a reason.

Then Angel came in, she sat beside me. Angel didn't speak, she sat quietly. I could hear her thoughts.

She wanted to tell me, how sorry she was, She wanted to tell me how beautiful we were together, and she wanted to tell me, she is here for me if I needed her.

I thought Angel was overly sweet, exceedingly kind and compassionate, just like her friend, my wife, Jewel.

I put my head down in my hands and covered my face. I wanted to cry, but I knew my tears would give me away.

I got up and left the room. I went back to my bedroom, took one look at my bed, and walked out of my bedroom slamming the door. I couldn't bring myself to go back in there. It hurt too much.

Kiss Of Life

I saw every memory of ours, flash before my eyes. That's when it hit me again.
I turned and went back into our bedroom.
I cried so much I didn't think I'd make the Wake. I punch the wall, putting holes in the, the size of small cars. I ripped apart my bed, and mutilated the bathroom, where Jewel's put her makeup on all the time.

I was never going to go back into that room on the fourth floor ever again.

Belvidere came running up to me. But I told him I needed to get it out of my system.

Belvidere told me to go wash up before someone saw me like this.

People started coming in to pay their respects to my Princess, leaving flowers on her Alter table and kissing her hands.

This went on for so many hours. All night immortals came and left. From everywhere.

Many of the spectators, asked to see me, but I couldn't be around everyone. I just wanted to sit next to Jewel's body alone. Mourn in my own way.

A few people found me, they Patted me on my back, they hugged me, and left gifts for me. Most of the time, I didn't even hear what was being said. They were talking to a Corp's themselves.

Then later, once the Castle was emptied of all the guests, I went in and sat with Jewel.
I couldn't understand why my Venom hadn't worked on her, turning her into a Vampire.
I inspected her body going over every spot I bit into Jewel. I still couldn't figure out what happen. I held her hands, her body was cold like mine. No blood flowing through her precious veins anymore. The warmth of her flesh was gone. One of the many things I loved about her.

I got up and walked around the Chapel, pacing back and forth trying hard to figure this out. What the hell went wrong.

I started to think it's her RARE BLOOD.
SHIT!
Now what?
She wouldn't be turned?

Kiss Of Life

After sitting next to Jewel, Tessa came into the Chapel, I could tell she cried some real tears of sorrow. She said to me, how she was going to miss her terribly, that Jewel was the only mortal that didn't care about Crowns and Titles. She was the real deal, the only one who cared more about people than her own self.

I thought about what she spoke, and for a minute I thought I felt my heart flutter with a beat, Tessa spoke the truth.

Then Belvidere came in, asking me if I was going to try to get some sleep. But I just looked at him, he told me, Jewel was like a daughter to me, and She will be missed like my child. My love for her will never cease.

Trevor came in next.
He didn't say anything for a long time. He just sat there staring up at Jewel. Tears of red, fell on his lap. Then he wiped them with his fingers and dried his hands on his slacks. He looked at me and said, in his deep voice in a mellow calming tone,

"This Fucking Sucks! I really liked her, and I feel terrible. Brook is so beside herself she's vomiting upstairs in the bathroom. *Brother*, I can't tell you enough how sorry I am, I wish there were something I could do."

Donna Tischner

He stood up, drying his hands on his trousers, then walked over to me, Trevor put his hand on my shoulder and grabbed me for a long hug, keeping us there for more than a few seconds.

I had to push him away...
He walked out of the Chapel.

I sat back down. I held Jewel's hand, there was no sound through out the whole Castle. Just quietness. It was a somber moment.

After some time, Brook entered the room.
Crying and wiping her eyes and nose. She stood behind my chair. Then placed both of her hands on the back of my shoulders, she bent down and wrapped her arms around my neck. Brook cried with her face in the crook of my neck, and I reached up, holding her hand. I pulled her around to me and held her as we both cried.

This is all my fault, she said. I'll never forgive myself. I'm so sorry Romanian. Crying and holding me tightly. I rubbed my hand over her head, her hair sticking to my bloody fingers. Brook didn't want to let go of me, but Trevor came back into the Chapel and pulled her off of me. She screamed in pain; wails of agony shattered through the house.

Then I heard some music in the background, The Scientist was playing by Coldplay, and my mind couldn't get a grip. I thought I was hearing things. I knew I had to figure this out.

Alfred stepped into my view, and he offered me some advice. He told me Jewels blood being so rare is not the reason she couldn't come back, it's because you don't believe. His hand reached for mine, and he took it placing it on Jewel's heart, then he told me, believe she's coming back to you! He shouted it like he was mad saying it again, "BELIEVE SHE'S COMING BACK TO YOU!" Alfred let go of my hand and walked out of the Chapel.

I thought about what he said, and I realized he's right.

The hours passed. It's been three days since my Princess went to sleep. I sat next to her body all night; I never left her side.

Soon immortals were coming back to the Castle to pay their respects.

Donna Tischner

This time it was, Misty and Lena. Their faces saddened my heart, seeing them covered in blood tears.

I stood there and watched as they lay over Jewel's chest. I walked over to the girls and placed my hands on their backs, They picked their heads up and turned to me hugging me.

This was bad...

I didn't realize how many Vampires loved her.

By night fall, I was still sitting next to Jewel. I spoke to her, telling her how much I love her, saying you're coming back to me now.

I sat down in my chair. I closed my eyes. More music played through out the Castle. This time it was,
The kiss of life by Sade.
The clock was ticking, and I knew, if she was going to come back it had to be now.

Everyone was in their rooms, no one around me. I stood up and closed the Chapel doors, then walked over to Jewel, I picked her up in my arms and held her.

Kiss Of Life

One single tear of my blood fell on her lips. I went to wipe it, but as I wiped her lips, I accidently pushed it into her mouth.

I apologized to her and bent over to kiss her. This was either going to be, *goodbye, or welcome back*.

As I kissed her again, I cried in her mouth puffs of air, not on purpose, I couldn't deal with this loss. My breath heaved, my tears fell, with my face embedded into her lips. I thought I heard something. I lifted my head watching her. Then I heard it again, her body was reforming, I squeezed her so hard, saying, "Princess, come on!" And somehow, her eyes opened. I started to shake; my excitement was too much. Her eyes followed mine. She looked right at me.

She kept her gaze on me for some time before saying, "What happen?"
I laughed so hard!
I held her and held her and kissed her. She said,
"Roman you're choking me." I laugh again. In my excitement everyone came running down slamming the doors open, staring, and watching as Jewel's sits up and smiles at everyone.

Donna Tischner

There was too much excitement. I didn't want to let go of Jewel, but everyone wanted to hug her. I lifted Jewel off the Alter and placed her feet to the floor. She stood a little wobbly, I held her arms so she wouldn't fall.

Brook grabbed her crying and hugging her. Even Alfred offered some tears of joy. It was heavenly.

I knew she was going to need to feed. There were too many mortals in the Castle, I had to get her out of there.

I asked everyone to step back, as I walked Jewel through the Castle. Taking her to feed.

She asked me, "Am I a Vampire now?" She was so cute. Her big brown eyes saddened by the news. When I answered saying, "We will be together forever now."

Jewel put her hand to my cheek and smiled saying, "You gave me the kiss of life, what more could I ask for. Being with you now, for eternity."

I reached up and held her hand on my face, calling her my Princess.

She fed. She kissed me. She loves me. What more could I

Kiss Of Life

ask for.

Soon I knew, I would have to teach her the ways of this life, she was ready and willing.

I kept her away from the Castle until she could stand being in a room with mortals, without wanting to rip them apart.

I said to her, "Printesa mea."
And she said to me, "My Princess." "Yes, that's right, That's My Princess in Romanian." I said.

Her kiss to my lips was like a child in a field of candy, it was that sweet. With my Princess back, life would only get better now. We're going to be unstoppable.

Jewel's grabbed me, and said I need you now. I felt my pulse rise and as the rain came down, I took her right there in the woods. The wind blew a breeze of fresh air and it flew over us, she moaned.

Her nails grazed my back as she bit into my neck, she was loving and savoring the extraction. Tasting my blood was new for her in this form, and she couldn't stop.

Jewel tilted her neck for me, and I bit into her. That sweet

Donna Tischner

blood ran through my veins and I felt her power run through my body.

Her eyes turned red like fire as she moaned and hissed at me in her great desire.
 There was no stopping her in this moment of pleasure.

I laughed and she kept going. Drinking my blood and loving my body.

This was new for me too; it has been decades since I felt power like this. Love like hers. This was real, what we have is special.

In no time she was filled with pleasure and demanded I hold her for the moment. I was enamored by my Jewel, her sweetness spilt into me and I was never going to let her go again.

After a few days in the woods, we made our way back to the Castle and we were greeted back with open hearts and smiles of satisfaction.

Kiss Of Life

Angel came to terms with Vampires being real and Brook had finally forgiven herself. Alfred would stay on with us and Belvidere was thankful to have his daughter home.

The End...

Donna Tischner

Thank you for taking your time to read my book.
XOXO

Kiss Of Life

About the Author

Donna Tischner has a
love for the arts.
Playing her piano and creating
art through oils on canvas.
She began writing romance novels in 2016.
She found it to be relaxing and exciting.
Donna enjoys sitting in her studio on her
Laptop bringing her stories to life.
Born and raised on Long Island, NY,
After her Breast Cancer diagnosis in 2013, having gone
through the worst parts of Chemotherapy, Radiation, and her
surgeries, she began listening to more music, she says,
"Sing every day, smile, and love life to the fullest.
Tomorrow isn't promised to us."
Her inspiration has inspired, as she pushes every
day doing what she loves.

Donna Tischner

"THIS BOOK IS BASED ON SOME TRUE FACTS..."

Kiss Of Life

©

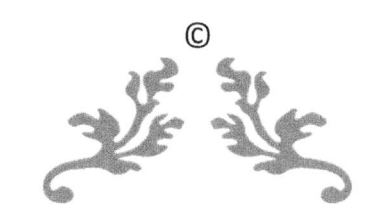

THE KISS OF LIFE

THE IMPOSSIBLE ROMANCE

DONNA TISCHNER

Donna Tischner